KOREATOWN BLUES

KOREATOWN BLUES

Mark Rogers

MARK ROGERS

BRASH
BOOKS

The characters and events portrayed in this book are fictitious. Any similarity to real persons, living or dead, is coincidental and not intended by the author.

ISBN: 1941298982
ISBN-13: 9781941298985

Published by Brash Books, LLC
12120 State Line #253,
Leawood, Kansas 66209

www.brash-books.com

For Sofia, who makes me want to be a better man.

ONE

As usual, I was the only white guy in the place.

I watched as the cordless microphone was passed down along the bar to Ban Gu, a pale-faced Korean with huge bags under his eyes. I looked up at the wall-mounted TV behind the bar. A Korean ballad began to play—words I couldn't understand. Ban Gu got deep into the tune—he was a good singer.

Once or twice, when I got really drunk, I'd try to sing in Korean. No one ever told me to shut up. No one ever grabbed the mic out of my hand. Instead they'd smile and slap me on the back as I gutted their language.

I looked over at the front door where a tall floor fan whirred and buzzed, doing its best to cool off the bar. Cars drove past. It took some getting used to—sitting in a bar and being on public view.

There was only an inch left in my bottle of Hite. At five bucks a pop I could only afford one or two a night. I looked up at the queue of songs running along the bottom of the video image. My song was next—I'd sing and then go home.

Ban Gu finished up, and Min Jee, the good-looking barmaid, took the mic out of his hand. She handed it to me with a smile. Min Jee had her hair dyed an auburn color, with streaks of blond highlights. She almost always wore golden earrings of some kind. For weeks now I'd been thinking of asking her out, but I always took a step back. I liked coming to the Saja Room every night for a song and a beer—I didn't want to do anything to fuck it up.

1

The first notes of "Moon River" began to play, and I looked up at the karaoke screen. I knew the lyrics by heart, but I liked the reassurance of seeing the words crawl slowly up the TV tube. The screen showed a flurry of disconnected Korean images unrelated to the song—a bungee jumper, animated cell phones, kids bouncing a ball, cherry blossoms waving in the wind—the images made no sense at all.

I weighed the mic in my hand. It had a lot of reverb, and it made almost every singer sound like he was in the shower, his voice bouncing off the tiles. There were a few singers the mic couldn't save—guys who sang angry, loud, and desperate. Most patrons would stare into their drinks when a singer like that roamed the floor—they rarely sang from their seats since they were in too much pain to sit still. But karaoke Korean style was all about flushing out the jimjams. It was no *American Idol* fantasy. It was a balm for the psyche.

I began to sing, enjoying the feeling. "Moon River" was my song. My grandma back in Pittsburgh used to play that tune over and over. It had gotten under my skin in an odd way, and when I first dropped into Saja and they handed me the mic, without thinking I asked for "Moon River." The regulars all had their signature song, and this was mine.

I glanced over at Ms. Tam, the owner of the bar. She was smiling. She liked it when I sang. The Koreans were middle class and were pleased when a white guy showed them respect—even a white guy like me, in jeans and a black T-shirt.

Ms. Tam looked to be in her fifties, still put together well, always wearing a sheath-like dress. I think her black hair was a wig, since it never changed shape. She always had a Marlboro pasted to her lower lip. The rest of LA had won the war against smokers, but you'd never know it in Koreatown. It seemed like everyone in Saja smoked—the air was blue with it. I didn't have the habit, but I breathed in so much secondhand smoke I'd probably have to start wearing a patch if I ever changed bars.

There was a young Korean woman standing next to Ms. Tam. I'd never seen her before. She kept her head down and leaned in toward Ms. Tam, like a shadow. Dressed in a white shift, she looked demure next to the older woman's flash. I'd noticed that most Korean women had a really hearty sensuality about them. This young woman looked bled out and shy.

I dug into the lyrics—about drifters and huckleberry friends and heartbreakers.

There was polite applause at the end of my song, and some of the patrons raised their beers in a salute. I gave a little wave of thanks and handed the mic to Min Jee.

Min Jee said, "I like the way you sing that song. So much feeling."

She brought the mic down to a gray-haired Korean, and the old guy started singing an upbeat number.

Maybe it was worth the risk, asking Min Jee out. Maybe there was a way I could approach it without feeling like a jerk if she said no. There was a fancy-looking Korean barbecue restaurant a block away. I could ask her to show me the ropes when it came to Korean cooking. I'd examined the menu on the front door a couple of times—it looked confusing as hell.

I was imagining sitting across from Min Jee, maneuvering a pair of chopsticks, eating something gooey and strange, when I saw a Korean dude walk into the bar. Instead of finding a seat, he stood in the open doorway. The guy had presence—a sense of style. He wore a sharp-looking suit without a tie; his glowing white shirt was open at the neck. He had the fresh look of a guy straight from the barbershop. It was strange the way he stood there, his eyes searching the bar. There wasn't much to see—just a long row of stools, a tiny dance floor, and a couple of restrooms off the kitchen. The guy's eyes fastened on Ms. Tam and the young woman standing close to her.

The man smiled—

Then his head exploded in a burst of shotgun fire from the street.

TWO

My ears rang as I crouched on the floor, trying to shield myself behind my bar stool. Half the patrons were screaming; the others were shocked into silence. Through the open doorway I saw a car roar off with the shooter leaning out the passenger's side. The well-dressed dude lay on the floor, flat on his stomach. Blood poured from what was left of his head.

I looked at the back of my hand and saw drops of blood. I felt my forehead and face, and there was blood there, too. I wasn't wounded—the blood had splattered over me. I started to shake. I climbed to my feet and held on to the bar with both hands. I looked around and saw what seemed to be every patron punching away at their cell phones, calling 911.

Min Jee was huddled behind the bar. She looked up at me and said, "The door. Please close the door. Lock it."

I carefully stepped around the body and closed the front door, throwing the bolt. Ms. Tam was trying to light a cigarette, looking grim. The young girl in white hid behind Ms. Tam, trembling.

A Korean guy named Kwan jerked his chin toward Ms. Tam and the girl. "It's all because of her."

I didn't understand what he was getting at, and asked, "Ms. Tam?"

"No," said Kwan. "The girl. Soo Jin. She's Nang. Nang family."

Min Jee leaned over the bar and handed me a damp towel. "Your face."

I took the towel and peered into the bar mirror, dabbing away at the blood on my forehead—and something that wasn't blood, something pulpy and white. I heard the sirens and walked over to the door and opened it. The cops would be pissed if they couldn't breeze right in. A crowd had gathered outside. They shouted some questions at me in Korean, but I ignored them and went back to my seat.

Seconds later the first cruiser pulled up to the curb, and the bar went dead silent. That's when I realized that all the police were going to get as far as testimony was a lot of "I don't know" and "I didn't see." And that's what happened. The police tried to get the story in English and got nothing much at all. When a Korean-speaking cop showed up, there was even less said.

One of the first two cops on the scene eventually got around to me. With a hand on my elbow he guided me back toward the corner of the bar, near the kitchen. He was a Latino with a rough complexion.

He glanced at the other patrons and then looked me in the eye. "What did you see?"

I told him exactly what I'd seen, leaving out the part about the car and the shooter.

He pointed at the body on the floor. "You ever seen this guy?"

"No. I don't think so."

He gave me a hard look. "What are you doing in this place?"

"Drinking beer," I said. "It's close to my apartment."

"What do you do?"

"I manage a car wash."

"I run you through the system, what am I gonna find?" asked the cop.

"Nothing. Not even a parking ticket."

He held out his hand. "Give me your ID."

He took my wallet and walked away.

I watched him make a call.

A few minutes later he came back with my wallet and handed it to me, saying, "A young guy like you hanging around here, with a bunch of bucketheads, I don't like it."

I kept my mouth shut. Growing up in Pittsburgh I learned early that the less said to cops, the better.

I walked over to Ms. Tam and the young girl I now knew was named Soo Jin. She was fresh-faced up close, delicate. She wouldn't look me in the eye.

"Ms. Tam," I asked. "You all right?"

I don't know why I asked her that—she was the toughest person in the room.

"Bad business," said Ms. Tam.

THREE

I watched my crew swarm over a green Honda Pilot, soaping it up and scrubbing it down before giving the signal to proceed through the car wash. You wouldn't find a Korean working at the Warsaw Wash. My crew was all Mexican—not one of them with papers. Hardworking guys who lived four to a room, sending most of what they earned back home to their families.

The Honda Pilot came through the car wash, and the driver stepped out, a tiny Korean lady. She took a seat in a row of chairs against the wall and watched as three workers buffed and dried her car, vacuumed the interior, and dressed her tires. When they were done she stuck a dollar in the tip jar and drove off.

A worker named Manuel, in rubber boots and black rubber apron, came over to me during a lull in the flow of cars.

Manuel bobbed his chin up and down. "So you were there, huh?"

"You talking about last night?"

"Yeah. At that karaoke club."

I looked out toward Western Avenue. "It was terrible. Bloody."

"You're lucky you didn't get shot, homes," said Manuel.

I nodded in agreement. "They say it was a shotgun."

"You ever be in the war?" asked Manuel.

"No," I said. "Never wanted to be, either."

Manuel said, "Why they didn't do that guy in the street? That stuff be *pinche*, shooting where they had women and all."

A car drove in, and Manuel drifted off to hose it down. I wondered if Saja would be open tonight, or if I'd find it sealed off with yellow crime scene tape.

LA may have been huge and sprawling, but my orbit was tight and contained. Saja was three blocks east of the car wash, and my apartment was two blocks north. I did my shopping at a Ralphs supermarket, one block west, and I got my reading matter and DVDs at the public library, right across from Ralphs.

I guess I wasn't much for new experiences. I'd only ever been in two places, really. I grew up in Pittsburgh. When I was nineteen a buddy of mine, Will, asked me to drive to LA with him. He was going to be an actor, and he wanted me to come along for moral support. There was nothing holding me in Pittsburgh so we drove straight across the country, taking turns driving and sleeping. Will only lasted eight months before he gave up on his dream and went back to enroll in a community college in Pittsburgh. I stayed on in LA—I had my job at the car wash. Six years later, I still had it. The only difference after Will left was I moved to the smallest apartment I could find, what they call a bachelor. It was one room and didn't have a kitchen, but that worked for me. I got along fine with a microwave, small refrigerator, and a Mr. Coffee.

A black Toyota Camry drove in to be washed. It was a gypsy cab belonging to one of my favorite customers—Yun, a Korean woman in her late thirties who worked twelve-hour shifts. I watched her get out of her car and walk back to where I was standing. She was wearing jeans, high-heeled sandals, and a burgundy Aéropostale T-shirt. She stood close to me—too close—and peered at my face. There was always a sexual charge coming off Yun. I knew she was married so it never went anywhere.

I took a step back and asked, "Why are you looking at me like that?"

Yun grinned. "They told me you had blood splashed all over your face. I was checking to see if you missed a spot."

Yun licked the tip of her finger and rubbed it lightly by the side of my lip. "There. That's better."

Yun was ten years older than me and always seemed ten steps ahead.

I said, "So you heard?"

"Lots and lots of talk," said Yun. "I'm glad you weren't hurt."

"No one got hurt. Just the poor guy who got his head blown off. Have you heard anything about them catching the guys who did it?"

"You know how it is in Koreatown," said Yun, looking away. "No one is going to talk."

The crew finished up with Yun's car. I noticed she had a photo of her kids taped to the dash.

Yun got behind the wheel and powered down the window. She gave me a serious look, unusual for her.

"I know you're gonna go back there," she said. "Be careful."

FOUR

It was five minutes to closing when the owner of the car wash showed up. It was unusual to see Jules in the middle of the week. He usually rolled in on Friday afternoon before the Sabbath. He didn't really have to come in at all, since he kept track of all the deposits online. Most of the business was cash, and he liked me to deposit it directly into a savings account at a Citibank a couple blocks away. He said he trusted me, but I also think he had his ways of knowing whether or not I was skimming off the cream. I'd been tempted in my early days at the car wash and had almost taken the plunge a couple of times. But I never did fall into the trap of taking what wasn't mine. The urge to steal from Jules eventually disappeared, and I settled into running his business the best I could.

Jules was an old-school Jew pushing seventy. His kids were grown and in solid professions. I'd had a few discussions with him about me buying the place. These talks always ended with Jules saying, "What am I gonna do if I retire? Sit on the couch and watch *Judge Judy*?" I had a feeling that was what he was doing already, since I only saw him once a week.

He had me over for dinner a couple of times, to his house in Redondo Beach. I think in some ways he considered me his working-class son—the one who was meant to inherit the family business.

Today he looked like he had something on his mind.

Manuel fastened the chain across the entrance to the car wash, a CLOSED sign dangling from the links.

Jules gestured toward the car wash garage doors. "Lock up and then come with me."

I secured the padlock. "Where we going?"

"Nowhere. For a sit in my car. I got something I want to talk about."

We walked over to his powder-blue Grand Marquis parked at the curb. We got in and he rolled down the windows to let in some air. Even this late in the day the heat was brutal.

"I never had a guy with me this long," said Jules. "One year—two, tops—and then they were gone. I don't know if that's a good thing or not. It's been good for me, you sticking around. But good for you, I'm not so sure."

I didn't like the sound of this, as though he was preparing to kick me to the curb. "I'm not complaining, Jules. This is what I do. I'm good at it. No one's going to give me any awards for doing it, but I'm fine with that."

"I've been at this location since seventy-two," said Jules. "It's been good to me. I'd like to see the right person get it."

"What do you mean?"

"I'm selling. I've got my reasons—some personal stuff with my wife. I don't want to get into it. But it's time to sell. You get first crack. But I'm a businessman—I'm not going to give it away."

This was happening too fast. I'd been saving for this day the last three years. Problem is I thought I had a few more years before Jules and I had this conversation.

"What's your price?"

"Two hundred K. But for you, I'll cut you a break on the down payment. Give me twenty-five grand and pay off a thousand a week and it's yours."

I had $9,000 saved. That was it. My car was an old beater, a 1999 Dodge Dart. I couldn't break a thousand selling it on Craigslist. The only thing I had that was worth any money at all was back in Pittsburgh, a 1970 Chevy Nova. I'd left it garaged at

my dad's house waiting for a day like today. It would sell overnight if the price was right.

I asked, "How much time can you give me?"

Jules looked disappointed by my question. "Not what I was
hoping to hear. Something like this, you either have it or you
don't."

"I've given you six years, Jules. Give me three days at least."

"I'll give you five days. Do what you have to do and then
we'll sign some papers." Jules pointed at the car wash. "That little
baby's been good to me. They can outsource the hell out of this
country, but they'll never be able to outsource plumbers, barbers,
and getting your car washed."

FIVE

The public library had a long bank of computers for patrons to use. But those computers you had to reserve in advance. Off in a corner was a lone PC that was available for only fifteen minutes at a time. This one you didn't have to reserve. The problem was it usually drew an odd group of users—street people and those who had an emotional screw loose.

I was next in line and waited for a guy in a suit to finish up. From time to time he'd glance over his shoulder at me in a pissed-off way. It was odd to see a guy in a suit at the free computer. Then I took a closer look and saw that the seam in the left shoulder of his suit jacket was starting to go, and his socks had lost their elasticity and were drooping around his ankles.

The third time he looked over his shoulder he snarled, "Do you mind?"

I said, "Mind what?"

"Giving me some privacy. You're breathing down my neck while I'm doing my banking."

I glanced down at my feet—I was standing behind the line of tape they'd stuck to the floor. "Hey," I said. "You want privacy don't do your business in a public library."

He looked down at the keyboard and muttered a low, "Jerk…"

A few minutes later the monitor's screen went black—his fifteen minutes were up. He walked away without looking back, and I sat down and signed in. In seconds I was on the Kelley Blue Book website, checking out what my 1970 Chevy Nova would be worth—up to $11,000. I checked some other sites for car collectors and found I could make a little more—it all depended on condition and how many of the original features were still intact. Then I took a whirl on Craigslist and got some encouraging numbers. My Nova was nowhere near cherry, but I could still net some good dollars. If I could unload it quickly, I'd be within passing range of the down payment Jules was looking for.

Back in my small apartment I stalled as long as I could. I took a shower. Ate a microwave burrito. Took out the trash. But I could stall only so long before making the call to my dad back in Pittsburgh. He was three hours ahead on the clock, and if his habits were the same, he'd be half-drunk by nine and asleep by eleven.

I hadn't called my dad for six months, and that had been the obligatory call on his birthday. The call had been short—before we got into anything real he was signing off with a "Thanks for calling" and then hanging up. I'd gotten used to it over the years. Mom died when I was fifteen, and my older brother, Steve, moved out as soon as he could, when he was seventeen. The seven years after my mom died, my father and I occupied the same house, but we rarely spoke to each other. The only meals we shared were accidental, when we happened to put plates of food on the table at the same time. I'd never gotten the feeling he loved my mom, his wife. But her death left a hole in his life that was filled with steady drinking and a diet of Fox News. The only time he got excited was when he repeated a nugget of wisdom from Bill O'Reilly or Sean Hannity. His job as a manager at Home Depot left him little to talk about. When I was eighteen I asked him if he could get me a job there, and his answer was, "I don't think it's a good idea."

The Chevy Nova had been Steve's car. He'd passed it down to me when it was in bad condition. I remember him telling me, "She has good bones, but she needs a lot of work." Over the years I'd fooled with it, bringing it back to running condition and keeping it clean.

I sat down in the one comfortable chair in my room—a black vinyl easy chair from IKEA that had been left behind when a tenant moved out of the building. I'd been the first to claim it from the lobby where it had a piece of paper taped to it with the message, "Take me."

I punched numbers into the phone, and my dad answered on the first ring.

"Hi, Dad, it's Wes."

There was a pause, then, "Are you all right? It's late to be calling here."

"Yeah, I know—I should have called earlier." This was met by silence on the other end. I picked up the slack and said, "I've got an opportunity out here. You know that car wash I've been working at? I've got a chance to buy it. My boss is retiring."

"You got that kind of money?"

"I've been saving. I've got some of the down payment on hand. I'm not asking for a loan from you or nothing like that. But I could use a favor."

"What kind of favor?"

"I'm going to sell the Nova. There may be some buyers coming by the house to give it a look and maybe even test-drive it. I think I can move it real quick. Hopefully it wouldn't be too much of a drain on your time, handling the sale."

There was another long pause, and then he said, "I sold that years ago."

"What?"

"I sold the Nova."

I felt like someone was squeezing my heart. "That was mine."

"It was Steve's. And where do you think he got the money for it?"

"No, Dad. That was my car. You didn't have the right to sell it."

"You left the fucking thing in my garage for six years. You're a man. You take care of your things. Take responsibility. Otherwise, you face the consequences."

"This isn't right."

"That's the way the cookie crumbles."

"Hey, you could've told me you didn't want it in your garage. I would have done something about it."

I heard laughter on the other end of the line, and then my father said, "You better do your push-ups—you'll be washing cars by hand the rest of your life."

SIX

A Korean was standing in the middle of the floor, singing into the cordless mic, mangling "Proud Mary," really struggling with the "Rs" in the "rolling on the river" line.

I held up my empty bottle of Hite and got Min Jee's attention. "One more."

I'd made a second call after my dad hung up on me, to my brother, Steve. When he picked up I could hear his two kids in the background and his wife yelling. I asked him about a loan, and his answer came back quick:

"No."

He didn't give me a reason, and I didn't ask for one.

Steve and I hardly ever spoke. He and his family lived in a town house apartment in South Jersey, where Steve worked for a trucking outfit. It was a sore point with him that I'd never been out to meet his kids. I sent presents at Christmas and for their birthdays, but he and I both knew that wasn't enough. Thing is, even before his kids came along, we rarely saw each other.

Our family was like a chemical compound: mix hydrogen and oxygen and you got water. Mix isolation and disinterest and you got my family. We could change things through an act of will if any of us cared enough. Thing is, we didn't. If Steve had called me for a loan, I doubt I would have parted with the nine grand I'd saved toward buying the car wash. I was no different from him. No different from my father. Asking for help came hard; refusing help came easy.

The singer finished the Creedence song with a strangled note that ended in a gurgle.

I hadn't been that surprised to find the Saja Room open after last night's bloody shooting. If it's one thing Koreatown understands, it's business. The flow of dollars must be kept open and constant. There was no time to mourn. Cart off the body, bag the evidence, and scrub away the blood. Do it fast—overnight if possible—so you can open the next day, pouring beer and soju and cranking out the karaoke.

And anyway, the guy who got his head blown off wasn't a regular.

Kwan came through the door and took the stool next to me. Kwan was different; he was a regular, maybe *the* regular. He not only drank in the Saja Room, he also ate there. While I kept my daily limit to two beers and a tip, Kwan probably dropped fifty bucks a night in the place.

Min Jee came over. Today her gold earrings were a leaf design that enfolded the lobes of her ears.

Kwan said, "Give me a Cass and an order of kimchi *jjigae*."

Min Jee put a beer in front of Kwan and walked off to the kitchen to place his order.

Kwan looked at the spot on the floor where the dead man had lain. "You wouldn't know he was ever there."

I asked, "Did you know the guy?"

"His name was Dae-Hyun. He drank at Radio Rose, on Olympic. I knew people who did business with him."

"He looked like a successful guy."

"What goes up must come down," said Kwan. "He had the car and clothes from the good days, but I heard he was having some troubles." Kwan glanced at Ms. Tam where she stood at the end of the bar. "That's why he came here."

I leaned in close to Kwan and spoke softly. "Ms. Tam gives loans?"

"No," said Kwan. "Ms. Tam gives nothing away."

I was confused, but that usually happened whenever I entered into a conversation in Saja. It was easier to just sing and drink.

Min Jee came back with a tray containing a bubbling stone crock of soup and a side order of rice. There was also a couple of tiny plates of pickled vegetables that reeked of garlic.

Kwan dug into his soup and then looked up at me. "Kimchi *jjigae*. This will put hair on your balls."

"Yeah, well…"

Min Jee asked if I was going to sing.

"I don't know," I answered. "Maybe. I still feel weird after last night."

Min Jee said, "Why don't you sing a song for the dead man, in his memory."

"I didn't know the guy."

"That shouldn't matter," said Min Jee.

I thought it over and then said, "Bring me the book."

Min Jee handed over a three-ring binder. It had an alphabetical listing of all the songs they had on their karaoke machine. Most of the songs were Korean, but they had a healthy selection of songs in English, going back to Sinatra and all the way up to bands like the Red Hot Chili Peppers and old-school rap like Ice Cube. I gravitated toward the ballads. I flipped through the binder and asked Min Jee to play 128997.

The first bars of my song began to play—"Help Me Make It Through the Night." Usually I thought about Min Jee or some other woman when I sang this song. Tonight it was disturbing—I thought about my dad, especially when I came to the line about yesterday being dead and gone.

After my song was finished, I walked back to the bathroom to take a piss.

It felt weird singing for a dead man. I didn't like the feeling. Most of the times I sang I thought of a young woman—a woman

I'd never met. Her features were indistinct. All I knew was she was the woman who was waiting for me.

When I came out of the bathroom, Ms. Tam was standing by the door.

She said, "I have a proposition for you. But I don't want to talk about it here."

She handed me a piece of paper with a Koreatown address on it. "Meet me at three o'clock. After I close."

I asked, "Three o'clock in the morning?"

"Yes." Ms. Tam's eyes held my own. "Will you come?"

SEVEN

I stood outside the address on Oxford Street, looking up at a concrete and steel apartment building, one of the newer builds on the block. The street was silent at this hour, three in the morning.

I wasn't sure what Ms. Tam had in mind. She had that Dragon Lady quality that aged well. Ms. Tam had a good twenty years on me, but it had been a while since I'd been in bed with a woman. I'd taken a shower, shaved, and put on clean underwear just in case she decided to seduce me. I was enjoying the fantasy, but I knew this had a slim chance of happening. Ms. Tam had some business in mind, maybe even something to do with the killing last night.

I entered the vestibule and pressed the button over her nameplate. A buzzer sounded and I pushed the door open. Ms. Tam was on the third floor so I rode the elevator up instead of taking the stairs. When I knocked on her door there was a pause as she looked through the peephole. The door swung open, and Ms. Tam gestured me to come inside.

I followed her down a hallway toward her dining room. Ms. Tam wore what she'd been wearing in the Saja Room—a green sheath dress of shiny material with sheer sleeves. I was glad she hadn't taken her wig off.

She motioned for me to take a seat. So far she hadn't said a word.

I sat down and looked around. I don't know what I'd expected to see in her apartment—probably something along the lines of ornate Oriental furnishings, decorated folding screens, brush paintings on rice paper. Instead the décor was sleek and modern—lots of glass, polished chrome, and black leather. A large painting of a roaring lion hung over the low-slung couch, and I remembered that *Saja* meant *Lion* in Korean.

Ms. Tam asked, "Would you like some tea?"

"Thanks. No milk, no sugar."

I listened to the soft clatter of cups being moved around and tea being poured. Ms. Tam reappeared and handed me a white LA Lakers mug. She drank from a mug with the Playboy logo.

"Green tea," she said.

We both sipped our tea. I kept silent. It was her call.

"I heard about Warsaw Wash."

"What'd you hear?"

"That it was up for sale."

Inside, my mind was churning. She was going to buy Warsaw Wash. I was going to be working for her. All my plans were circling the drain.

"I heard another rumor on the street," said Ms. Tam. "Whispers. Everyone in Koreatown knows everybody else's business. We pretend to be very private. I hate the Japanese for calling us monkeys, but sometimes we chatter like monkeys."

I took a sip of tea and waited for her to say more.

Ms. Tam said, "I also heard that you want to buy Warsaw Wash."

"Yeah, that's true."

"I see you come in every night. You walk to the bar. You buy one beer, maybe two. You wear jeans and a T-shirt. When I heard you wanted to buy Warsaw Wash, I thought, How does Wes have the money?"

"I guess I have a little Korean in me," I said. "I save."

Ms. Tam pressed her thin lips into an even more compressed line. "Say you have the money for the down payment. And I wonder if you do. But say you have it. Owning a business has many hidden costs. Have you ever owned a house?"

"No, I haven't."

"When you buy a house you find yourself with a new set of expenses. Plumber. Insurance. Taxes. All kinds of things. It's the same with a business."

"I hope I have a chance to find out about all these new expenses," I said. "But to cut this short, I'm not looking for a partner."

Ms. Tam smiled. "I don't want to own a car wash."

I reached out with my right hand and warmed my fingers on the mug. "I like you, Ms. Tam. But I'm beginning to feel like you're jerking me around."

"One moment," Ms. Tam said, standing up.

I watched her disappear down a short hallway. I heard a door open. Moments later Ms. Tam reappeared, with Soo Jin right behind her.

I stood up, the way you do when a lady enters the room.

Ms. Tam said, "I don't think you've been formally introduced. This is Soo Jin. Soo Jin, meet Wes."

I nodded, not sure if I should shake hands. Soo Jin looked diaphanous in a pale-blue dress that hung from her slim shoulders.

Ms. Tam and Soo Jin sat down, and I took my seat again.

"Your finances are your business," said Ms. Tam. "I'm not here to pry. I'm here to make you an offer."

EIGHT

The day had gone by in a blur. I'd only managed an hour or two of sleep before I had to show up at the car wash. All day my workers looked at me funny. One moment I'd be riding high, laughing and cracking jokes; the next minute I'd be silent, off by myself, brooding. I knew I was acting weird. But I couldn't help it. Life had taken a weird turn.

When we closed up at six I went straight back to my apartment. I took a hot shower and went to my clothes closet. I only had one suit. I don't think I'd worn it more than twice in two years. I took out a white shirt and a red tie with a paisley design. Dug around in the bottom of the closet for my dress shoes.

Only a few hours ago, at our predawn meeting, Ms. Tam had offered me $15,000 to marry Soo Jin. Combine Ms. Tam's offer with the 9K I had saved, and I was within a thousand of Jules's asking price for the down payment on the car wash. The offer put my mind into a spin. All of a sudden, the air in Ms. Tam's living room felt too close, too hot. I had stood up and said, "Give me a few minutes—I'll be right back with an answer."

I'd walked around the block a half dozen times, wishing there was a coffee shop open. What did I know about being married? I had faint, faint thoughts of getting married someday—maybe. It was lonely out on the street in the darkness and at times my footfalls would echo against a building's wall. Maybe that did it. Hearing those footsteps.

Ms. Tam buzzed me back in.

Ms. Tam stood in the center of the room. Soo Jin sat at the table.

"So?" asked Ms Tam.

I sensed desperation in Ms. Tam's voice, and I told her I couldn't do it for less than twenty. I was thinking of what she said about unexpected expenses—it would be nice to have a cushion. During the negotiations, Soo Jin had stared down at her folded hands on the table. She hadn't said a word since coming out of the bedroom.

I'd just agreed to marry her, and she still hadn't looked me in the eye.

Ms. Tam wasn't fazed by my demand for 20K. She said, "We can do twenty."

She got up and walked over to a cabinet and returned with three small glasses and a bottle of soju, a fiery Korean liquor distilled from rice.

"I think we should celebrate," said Ms. Tam, pouring soju into all three glasses.

We lifted our glasses. I drank it down in one shot and noticed Soo Jin only took a tiny sip. Good thing. Downing the whole thing might have knocked her out.

"I've heard about these arranged marriages," I said. "I'm going to have to know a lot of details about Soo Jin's life. Immigration is going to ask us a lot of questions. Intimate stuff, like what side of the bed she sleeps on, what kind of shampoo she uses. They're going to try to trick us. We're also going to need photos of us going to the beach, traveling, family events—all kinds of stuff."

Ms. Tam shook her head. "You won't need any of those things."

"Why?"

"Because Soo Jin is an American citizen. She was born here."

This wasn't making sense. "If she's a citizen, why are you paying me to marry her?"

"Because you are white," said Ms. Tam. "Maybe they will be afraid to kill you."

* * *

The whole story had come out slowly. The man who had been shotgunned the night before had been Soo Jin's suitor. He didn't make it past the introduction.

I listened as Ms. Tam told me the tale of a blood feud between the Nang and Doko families. It had begun in the homeland, in Busan and had emigrated to LA's Koreatown. It had been going on for generation after generation. The Doko family had vowed to keep all of the women of the Nang family childless. It was a war of attrition, and one would-be husband after another had been scared off, paid off, or cut down. Soo Jin was the only Nang woman left of childbearing age. It had taken a brave man—maybe a desperate man—to agree to marry Soo Jin, and he'd had his head blown off after setting eyes on her for the first time. When I asked Ms. Tam if these people are so ruthless, why don't they cut things off at the source and kill the women, she explained that there was an unwritten law of the feud, that the women of the family cannot be killed.

Ms. Tam had said, "Soo Jin is a ghost. No Korean man will marry her now."

I looked at Soo Jin. If she was the last woman left capable of bearing a child, I didn't hold out much hope for the Nang family. She looked too frail and pale to conceive, let only carry a child full term.

I thought about my dad telling me I was a loser, about my brother turning his back on my plea. I was on my own.

I was white. The Koreans weren't going to fuck with me.

I reached over and drank what was left in Soo Jin's glass. I set the glass down on the table with a knock and said, "Give me twenty-five thousand and you've got yourself a deal."

NINE

I stood in Ms. Tam's living room, wearing my suit and tie. Soo Jin was by my side, dressed in a pale-yellow shift and white high heels. I was wondering if anything less than pure white signified the same thing in her culture as it did in ours. If I had to put money on it, I'd have to bet she was a virgin. I also wondered if she was anemic. It was hard to imagine her sitting down to a grilled steak and a baked potato; Soo Jin looked more the type to dine on consommé and a mixed greens salad.

We still hadn't said more than two words to each other. A few days ago it would have blown my mind, my taking part in an arranged marriage. Now it just seemed expedient. The quickest path from A to B, with B being me owning Warsaw Wash.

Ms. Tam sat on the sofa next to Kwan, who for a fee had agreed to be the witness. Ms. Tam had assured Kwan he wouldn't be in danger acting as witness to the wedding, but he still demanded $200 and a week's worth of free dinners at the Saja Room.

In front of us stood a Korean justice of the peace. As he droned on in Korean my mind began to wander. I wondered what my father would think when he heard I was the sole owner of the car wash, that I had managed to ace the deal on my own. I almost wished Warsaw Wash was in Pittsburgh on a busy avenue, so my father would have to drive by every once in a while. It still stung inside—not so much that he had unloaded my Nova, but the glee he took in putting me down.

"Wes…Wes," said Ms. Tam. "Now you say, 'I take Soo Jin as my lawfully wedded wife.'"

I repeated what Ms. Tam asked, and repeated a few more phrases. Then the justice of the peace said in his first and only words in English, "You may now kiss the bride."

I looked into Soo Jin's eyes—she didn't seem scared. I was not movie-star material, but my face didn't frighten small children, either. The one attribute I had that I knew scored positive was my blue eyes. The Mexican women I encountered and the random Korean in the Saja Room enjoyed pointing them out, usually with a comment that I'd father cute blue-eyed babies. I took my blue eyes for granted, but I knew they were currency in some ethnicities.

I leaned in and gave Soo Jin a chaste kiss. You would have needed a seismograph to measure the delicacy of her response. No chance of earthquakes there.

I placed a gold band on Soo Jin's finger, supplied by Ms. Tam. Soo Jin did the same for me. The justice of the peace didn't waste any time and was out the door before Ms. Tam was done fiddling with an iPod in a docking station. She got some music playing—something Korean and lighthearted.

Ms. Tam pointed at Soo Jin and said to me, "You have to dance with the bride. It's your tradition. Soo Jin will have to learn your ways, the same you'll learn hers."

"Yeah, Wes," said Kwan. "She's your wife now. Hold on tight and have some fun."

I took Soo Jin by the hand and put my right hand on her slender waist. As we shuffled around the room I could feel the bones of her rib cage under her flesh—it made me think of the framework of a house. When I looked down I saw her eyes averted. My foot knocked against hers, and she stumbled a bit. I tightened my hold and kept her from looking too clumsy. She smiled at me—the first time she smiled in my presence. Her teeth were tiny, her tongue a bright pink.

The song ended and I let her go.

Soo Jin drifted back to stand next to Ms. Tam. It was an awkward moment, broken by Kwan popping the cork on a bottle of champagne. He poured four glasses and passed them around.

Ms. Tam said, "You make the toast, Kwan. You're the one who loves to talk."

We held our glasses high as Kwan said, "May you survive. May you live. May you be safe. May the shotguns never find you."

TEN

I took a right turn onto Western Avenue. Soo Jin was by my side. It felt strange wearing a suit and tie as I drove my old Dodge Dart. I felt like a down-on-his-luck salesman selling something nobody wanted.

When I took the turn I looked in my rearview mirror and saw an orange Jeep Rubicon pull into traffic right behind me. Maybe I was paranoid, but the Jeep had been behind me ever since Soo Jin and I left Ms. Tam's place on Oxford. It had to be paranoia on my part—who would tail someone in an orange Jeep Rubicon? It didn't make sense. It was the money. The money was making me nervous.

I hung a left on Olympic and drove into the huge Bank of America parking lot. I chose a space as close as I could to the bank of ATMs.

I patted Soo Jin on the knee. "I'll be a minute."

I got out and walked over to the deserted row of ATM machines. I looked around for the orange Jeep and didn't see it. I was jumpy. I had a right to be.

I fed my card into the ATM and punched deposit. I took a thick envelope out of my jacket pocket and began to feed hundreds into the machine—it was going to take me seven deposits to securely deposit the 25K into my account. Ms. Tam had given me the option of coming back the next day and picking up my payment during daylight hours, but I was too jacked to wait. I wanted to see that deposit slip with the big numbers. I'd have coffee with Jules tomorrow and make the deal—write him a check, give him a money order, hand over the cash—whatever made him happy.

I got back behind the wheel and pulled into traffic. I glanced over at Soo Jin and said, "This is a strange thing to ask, since we just got married—but do you speak English?"

Soo Jin said in a soft voice, "Yes."

"I'm not a big talker myself," I said. "Do you think they're going to try and kill me?"

"I don't know," said Soo Jin, staring straight ahead. "In my family, we were all Korean. No one ever married outside the race."

I braked at a red light. "Tough times, tough decisions."

I'd been so preoccupied with getting the down payment for the car wash and getting my tie on straight I'd glossed over an important detail: the Nang family wasn't paying me to marry Soo Jin; they were paying me to give her a child. The make-pretend marriage was no big deal to me. But how do you deal with a make-pretend fatherhood? No kid deserves that.

I looked over at Soo Jin again—at her delicate profile, glossy black hair, the slim curves of her body. It had been a couple of months since I'd been in bed with a woman, and that had been on a massage table and had cost me $125. The masseuse was a Korean woman with a Cesarean scar and an appealing over-bite. The sex had been explosive and perfunctory; the emotions tamped down and probably nonexistent on her part.

I wasn't proud that I sometimes paid for sex, but I knew why I did it. They've done studies on chimpanzees dying from the lack of touch. My mom had been the hands-off type. It didn't make that much of an impression on me until I was a thirteen-year-old at my first school dance. It only took one slow song with my hands wrapped around a girl to clue me in on what I'd been missing. Now, instead of withering on the vine and becoming even more strange, I budgeted money for an occasional massage and a screw. It wasn't the real thing. I didn't pretend it was the real thing. But without it—given my serious lack of game—I'd have no sex life at all.

We were a block from my apartment building. I looked in the rearview, and there was the orange Jeep Rubicon, two cars back.

There was no traffic ahead of me. The Jeep swung into the oncoming lane, roared past, and then turned back into the right lane. The Jeep slowed down to a crawl in front of me and then pulled into a parking space next to a hydrant, directly in front of my apartment.

I hung a right and turned into an empty space. I looked back at the Jeep—no one was getting out.

I pointed and asked, "Soo Jin, see that Jeep back there? Do you know anyone with a Jeep like that?"

Soo Jin looked back and said, "No."

"They've been following us since we left Ms. Tam's."

Soo Jin's features took on a saddened, downcast quality. Maybe she liked me a little bit and was imagining my head being blown off. Maybe she was just sorry for herself and the blood feud she'd been born into.

"C'mon," I said. "Everyone's been telling me they won't kill a white guy. Let's see how true that is."

I got Soo Jin's tartan plaid suitcase from the back seat and locked up the car. Soo Jin and I walked slowly toward the entrance to the apartment building, where the Jeep was parked. The night was warm. I could smell the smog, but it was something I'd grown accustomed to. I touched my cell phone in my pocket, wondering how fast I could dial 911. If we made it home tonight, I'd put 911 on my list of contacts.

I looked at Soo Jin. "You know, I didn't tell you, but you look very pretty tonight."

I couldn't see that clearly in the dim light, but it looked as though she was blushing as she smiled. "Thank you. You are very handsome."

The Jeep's headlights flashed on and then off. There looked to be four guys sitting inside the Jeep, but it was too dark to make out any details.

When we were a couple steps away the window powered down.

I stopped in my tracks.

A hand reached out and tossed a small box onto the sidewalk in front of us.

The window powered back up and the Jeep's engine turned over. It slowly drove off, disappearing around the corner.

I picked up the small box from the sidewalk:

Magnum Spermicidal Condoms.

ELEVEN

turned on the lights in my apartment. I hadn't had much time to prepare the place for Soo Jin. During my lunch hour I'd driven down Western Avenue and bought a cheap folding bed and some extra blankets. I also consolidated a few drawers and made space in the closet so she could have somewhere to put her stuff. At least the place was tidy—I guess you could say I was the opposite of a hoarder. I looked it up once. It's called Obsessive-Compulsive Spartanism. Everything in it place.

I put the suitcase on the bed and said, "I guess we'll pick up the rest of your stuff tomorrow."

Soo Jin's gaze was moving around the room, taking in the cramped quarters, the single bed, the midget refrigerator, the pile of biographies from the library. Even though I'd lived here over five years I could move out of the apartment in an hour. My living quarters suited me, but to anyone else it probably looked sad.

I asked, "Would you like some tea?"

Soo Jin nodded, and I put a cup of water in the microwave. As the water heated up, to reassure her I opened up the folding bed.

I pointed at the single bed. "I think that one will be more comfortable for you. It's got clean sheets and a clean pillowcase."

I opened the closet. "You've got space and hangers in here, and you can have the top two drawers in the dresser."

Soo Jin opened her suitcase. The microwave dinged, and I asked, "How do you like your tea?"

"Just tea," said Soo Jin.

I handed her the cup. "Do you have a job you have to go to?"

"I work in the Koreatown Plaza.

"That's close. You can walk."

"I work at Pao Jao. Ten to seven."

This was the first time she offered any information without being asked.

"What's Pao Jao?"

"Dumplings. All kinds."

I watched as Soo Jin put her things away. She took out a small toiletry bag and hesitated before going into the bathroom.

I looked at the clock radio by the side of the bed. 10:24. I never went to bed this early, although something told me it would be the smart thing to do. I prepared the folding bed on the far side of the room from Soo Jin's bed. I usually slept naked, but tonight I'd keep my boxers and T-shirt on.

Soo Jin came out of the bathroom and sat at the table, drinking her tea.

I pointed at the TV and DVD player. "I don't have cable. Just DVDs."

She looked disappointed. "No TV?"

"They have a lot of Korean movies at the library. I'll take you over there tomorrow."

Soo Jin nodded.

I got up. "I'm going to sleep early tonight."

I washed up. When I came out, Soo Jin was rinsing out the tea mug.

I sat on the edge of the folding bed and watched her go into the bathroom. I switched off the light and got under the covers. The folding bed was pretty bad—my feet hung over the end if I straightened out.

When Soo Jin came out of the bathroom my eyes were adjusted to the dark. Bars of light came into the room from the streetlight on the corner. Soo Jin looked lovely in a light night-gown. Then she was under the covers herself.

I drifted off, wondering what I'd just done.

TWELVE

I was used to eating in pho noodle shops and by the side of taco trucks. It felt strange to be in an all-American-type diner, looking down at a plate of eggs, rye toast, and a ceramic cup steaming with black coffee.

Jules and I were on Catalina Avenue in Redondo Beach at ten thirty in the morning, having just come from his lawyer's office, where I'd handed Jules a bank draft for 25K. In return, we signed the documents that turned Warsaw Wash over to me, provided I kept up with my payments. It was my goal to double up and own it lock, stock, and barrel in under two years.

"I have confidence in you," said Jules. "Being an owner is different than being a manager, but you know what you're doing."

"How different?"

"First of all, don't play around with your taxes—no more than you have to," said Jules, wagging his finger at me. "It's the quickest way to go into the tank. Second, don't carry a lousy employee, no matter how much you like him. In the long run you won't be doing either one of you a favor."

"You ever hire women?"

Jules's bushy eyebrows raised. "Bikini car wash? The quickest way to go out of business. Stick with the Mexicans. They're fucking Apache warriors—they can go all day."

"I'm thinking of making Manuel my manager."

"Big mistake," countered Jules. "Be a manager-owner for at least a year. Groom Manuel to fill in for you if you get sick or something. But the first year, plan on working six days a week. First one in, last one out."

"I got Manuel opening today."

"Do what you got to do but be the boss."

Jules tucked into his pastrami and eggs.

I took a sip of coffee.

Jules looked up. "Warsaw Wash was good to me. It'll be good to you, too."

* * *

I kept quiet the rest of the day, managing the car wash as though nothing had happened. My workers didn't know I was the new owner. At four in the afternoon, during a lull in the action, I gathered them around and asked if they could stay a few minutes after closing, that I had some news. This was met with frowns from most of them, and I realized that news for these guys was more often than not bad.

I walked over to Ralphs supermarket and picked up a case of ice-cold Tecates. When the last car was washed and the chain was secured across the entrance, I broke out the beers and handed them around to the six workers.

Manuel gave me a nervous look. "Wes. Are we gonna get in trouble with the boss, drinking beers?"

"No," I said. "Know why? Because the boss is going to drink with you."

I picked up a can of Tecate and popped the top. I held the can up and said, "To the new owner of Warsaw Wash. Me."

After it sunk in they let out a cheer. Manuel let fly with a full-throated mariachi "Ai yi yi yi yi!" A couple guys clapped me on the back. I explained that Jules had sold the business to me. I also reassured them that nothing much would change, since we'd been virtually running the place on our own.

Manuel turned up the music on our battered portable radio, and banda pumped loud. The guys raided the communal tip jar, and Ramon, a tiny guy with a carefully razored movie-star mustache, dashed across the street for a bottle of tequila.

I was into my second beer and third shot of tequila when I saw Yun's black Camry pull to a stop at the curb. She got out with a big smile on her face and yelled, "You're having a party and you didn't invite me?"

I waved her over. She looked good in low-slung khaki shorts and a pink T-shirt. I handed her a beer, and she asked, "Whose birthday is it?"

"Nobody's," I said. "I just bought the place. I'm working for myself now."

Yun smiled and gave me a hug. She didn't let go right away. I could smell the camellia scent in her hair. A fresh banda song began to play, and Manuel chanted, "Dance…dance…dance!"

Without letting go, Yun handed her beer to one of the workers and started in with the simple but fast banda step. I wasn't a great dancer, but I'd been to enough Mexican backyard barbecues to keep up with the beat. I don't know where Yun learned, but she was smooth and followed my lead as though we'd been practicing weeks for this moment.

You can dance the banda grandmother style, or as sexy as a lambada. Yun was holding on tight and had managed to get my leg firmly in between her thighs. My hand gripped low on her back and her pink T-shirt rode up, until my bare hand was on the flesh curving up from her round ass. I started to get hard, which didn't seem to faze Yun at all. The guys were letting out whoops, happy that a good-looking woman had joined the party. I didn't want the song to end, but it did. Yun gave me a kiss on the cheek and said, "Congratulations…"

Then she was gone, back in her car, on the way to pick up her next passenger.

Manuel handed me a plastic shot glass of tequila and said, watching Yun drive away, "Homes, that woman is a hundred and ten proof."

My body was still carrying a sexual charge. I really didn't know a lot about Yun. I knew she had a couple of young kids, and I'd heard her husband was a dour guy with the unfortunate name of Suck-Chin. She'd told me he'd moved to Boulder to take care of his ailing mother—that he'd been gone for over a year. There was zero warmth when Yun talked about her husband, but I knew Korean women were loyal to the max, and divorce was a last resort for most Koreans. Even if Suck-Chin was a pain in the ass Yun would stick by him.

But I could tell when a woman liked me. You can tell a lot by the way a woman dances with you. I've had women hold me at arm's length and talk a blue streak—anything to avoid having our bodies touch. Then there was Yun, who by the end of the dance had me tangled up in the sheets. Maybe she was playing a game, but it sure felt real to me.

Then I saw it—driving by on Sixth Street—the orange Jeep Rubicon. The window was down. An arm extended out with the hand cocked like a gun. The hand pointed at me and mimed firing, then mimicked the motion of a gun's recoil. I watched as the Jeep rolled on down the road, breezing through the amber traffic signal.

Manuel had seen the whole thing. He said to me, "Homes, you're the boss now. And like they say in the storybooks, heavy lies the head wearin' the crown."

THIRTEEN

When I got home I glanced at the clock and saw that it was almost seven. Soo Jin would be home soon.

I'd lived alone for a long time. It was going to take some getting used to sharing my small space with another person. Alone, the room didn't seem so small; I could disappear into my mind, or into a book or a DVD. With another person in the room it was going to resemble what it really was—a cage or a cell.

The guys at Warsaw Wash had chipped in for a bottle of champagne. I made space in the tiny refrigerator and placed it inside to keep it cool. At first I thought they might have heard I was married and the champagne was for me and Soo Jin to celebrate. I'm not sure why exactly, but I hadn't mentioned the marriage to them. I figured they might have heard something from a customer. Then, when they presented the bottle to me and congratulated me again on buying the car wash, I knew my private life was still private. Maybe I'd tell them tomorrow, after I'd had the chance to wrap my own head around the new change in my life.

I looked at the stack of books from the library. I tended toward biographies of successful people, it didn't matter their field of expertise. One day it might be Steve Jobs, the next day Jay Z. I took down the one I was currently reading, a bio of Colin Powell. I'm not sure what it was I was looking for in wading through these books. I think at least a little bit of it was related to the common-sense observation a high school English teacher had shared, that people judge you by the company you keep.

I was just getting relaxed when I heard the buzzer. I buzzed back, and in a minute or so Soo Jin appeared at the door, looking hesitant to even come in. She got up her nerve and stepped across the threshold. She was holding a white paper sack.

I took a step back. "Come on in."

I dug into my pocket and came up with two shiny keys. "I had these made for you today. You won't have to buzz yourself in anymore."

Soo Jin nodded her thanks and placed the bag on the table. "*Mandoo*. Dumplings from work. For our dinner."

I watched her set plates on the table. She'd brought disposable chopsticks and some packets of soy sauce. She set the dumplings on the plates and opened a second carton containing a green glob.

I pointed. "What's that?"

"*Sigeumchi namul.*"

"Yeah, but what is it?"

She smiled. "Spinach."

We ate in silence. When I'd polished off my dumplings, Soo Jin lifted a dumpling from her plate and put it on mine.

The sun was down and the lights were low. I watched Soo Jin clear away the dishes. I still had a buzz from the tequila a couple of hours ago, and the memory of holding Yun close during the dance was hovering at the edge of my consciousness.

I said, "Do you know why I agreed to marry you?"

Soo Jin wiped a plate dry and put it away. "You needed money for your business."

"My car wash."

"Maybe I could help you there."

"You know, I never saw a woman working at Warsaw Wash. But who knows? If I make a success of things maybe I'll have a job that a woman could do."

"A woman could wash cars."

"You're right. A woman could do anything a man can do. But believe me, if you have a better option than washing cars by hand, take it. It's hard work."

Soo Jin sat back down across from me and did her damnedest to look me in the eye and then looked down at the table. "I don't want you to die."

"That would be a drag."

"Even though the car wash would be mine, I still don't want you to die."

I hadn't thought about that. "No sense in killing me yet," I said. "The car wash is carrying a big mortgage. It'll be a couple of years before it's reached its full value. I'm the golden goose in this equation."

I switched on the clock radio and got some music, reggaeton from a Spanish station. I turned it down low—I just needed some noise in the room. I felt like Soo Jin was an empty vessel. If I raised her to the light I'd be able to see right through translucent flesh, blood, and bone.

To break the silence I walked over to the mini fridge and took out the bottle of champagne. Holding it up to Soo Jin, I said, "Last night we celebrated a wedding. Today we celebrate Warsaw Wash."

I took down a couple of glasses and popped the cork. I handed a glass to Soo Jin and said, "*Kampai.*"

"*Kampai,*" answered Soo Jin, before she took a small sip.

I sat down in the black vinyl chair, the bottle of champagne next to me on a folding table. Soo Jin sat on the edge of the bed. She was dressed in a simple white blouse and black slacks and was wearing what looked to be black ballet slippers. My head was swimming even as I gulped more champagne. That was my wife over there. The curves were subtle, but there was a woman under those simple clothes.

I asked, "Do you like me?"

"I don't know yet."

"How old are you?"

"Twenty-seven."

I would have pegged her for being much younger. "And you've never been married?"

"I've been married five times," answered Soo Jin. "Always to Korean men. They call me an old maid. But I am really an old widow."

"These husbands were all killed?"

"Yes. By the Doko family. My father thought they would never bring the blood feud all the way from Busan to Koreatown. But it wasn't true. Now I'm the last woman in the family young enough to have a child. They are erasing my family."

Soo Jin took a sip of champagne. I killed what was in my glass and refilled it to the brim.

"None of these husbands gave you a child?"

"They didn't live long enough."

"But you're not a virgin?"

Soo Jin blushed and looked away, not answering.

I heard a siren from the street and the sound of police copters overhead. On the radio, the singer was going on about "*perro*" this and "*perro*" that. Even not speaking much Spanish it was easy to figure what he was singing about, some kind of doggy-style reference. I got up and looked out the window and saw two cop cars hurtling past, red lights flashing.

I asked, "You allergic to candles?"

"No."

The previous tenant had left behind some tall candles in glass jars embossed with pictures of the Virgin Mary. I'd put them away under the sink. I got them out now and lit them up with a kitchen match. The candles lent the room a warm glow, but I saw Soo Jin tremble a little.

I poured another glass of champagne. The combination of Jimador, Tecates, and Freixenet was playing with my vision. "Do you think they're going to kill me?"

"The Doko family sees success very close now," said Soo Jin. "If they could, they would kill me. I'm sure they light Buddhist joss sticks hoping I get sick or have an accident. Killing you would make things difficult for them. I think first they will try to scare you."

I remembered Yun, my fingers on the smooth skin of her back, and I said to Soo Jin, "Are you my wife?"

"Yes."

"Are you cold?"

"A little."

I closed the window, even though the night was warm. I switched off the lamp in the corner. The room was now only illuminated by the pale light from the street and the meager glow from the candles, their Virgin Mary images animated by flickering flames.

I undid the buttons of my shirt.

Soo Jin watched me and then bent to take off her shoes. I watched as she slipped the blouse from her shoulders and pulled her pants down from her slim hips. She wore a white bra and panties that looked a size too big. Her hands bent around her back and she undid her bra, laying it on top of her blouse and pants. She was lovely, pale, and luminescent in the candlelight. The nipples of her breasts were so dark they were almost black.

I took off all of my clothes and walked over to the side of the bed, already erect. I bent and gently pulled her panties down her legs and placed them with her other clothes. I'd only kissed her once and had only held her in a brief wedding dance.

Soo Jin lay back, her legs slightly open, her eyes closed. She was my wife. My fingers trailed along her thigh. I kissed and caressed her, and nature took its course. She parted her legs wider, and I slipped inside.

It was like fucking a ghost.

She lay there without moving, her eyes closed as I took my pleasure, grinding away. My hands clasped her shoulders, and I felt as though she were disappearing into the bed. There had been too much fear. Too many dead husbands. She was dead inside.

I stopped in midstroke—hung there. But it was too late—a red pulse carried me over the edge, and I came inside her.

I felt ugly, like a beast.

I got up, my mouth dry from the champagne. I could feel a headache coming on.

Soo Jin's eyes opened.

I looked down at her, lying there on the bed.

I said, "I'm sorry."

I walked away, uncomfortable being naked. I pulled out the folding bed and got under the covers. Lay down with my face to the wall.

But I couldn't sleep.

FOURTEEN

My thumb scratched at the label on my bottle of Hite, digging a trail from top to bottom. I thought about Soo Jin alone in the apartment, and I wondered what she was thinking. She was no virgin. Even so, I felt as though I had violated her. It wasn't rape. It wasn't sex with a minor. Soo Jin was a woman made of glass. Not that she broke easily or that she was pure. It was more like she was clean and empty like a fresh-from-the-box test tube. Making love to her made me feel like a piece of meat, stinking with blood and hair.

Most days I liked myself. Tonight, not so much.

Min Jee handed me the microphone, and I looked up at the TV screen as my song began to play, a song the Silver Fox—Charlie Rich—made famous, about loving his woman behind closed doors.

When the song ended I handed the mic back to Min Jee.

She was looking at me funny—in fact, no one had given me a straight look since I came into the Saja Room. When I entered, the place was full—now it was half-empty.

Kwan was sitting three stools down, a full meal and a glass of soju in front of him.

I said, "Hello down there…"

Kwan looked up from his plate of barbecued ribs. "I should be eating in one of the booths."

"Why?"

"Because if they come in with a shotgun, I won't be in their range of fire."

I killed the bottle of Hite and waved for another. I said to Kwan, "You'd cry like a baby if I was gone."

Kwan gave me a sour look. "For about one day."

I got up and moved down next to him, so I wouldn't have to shout. "I have a feeling I'm bad for business."

Kwan dug a plastic toothpick out of his shirt pocket. "You should strike a deal with Ms. Tam. Maybe she would pay you not to drink here."

I looked over at Ms. Tam, where she sat in a high-backed stool behind the far end of the bar. Her face was impassive. She hadn't said a word to me about the wedding or Soo Jin.

I said to Kwan, "Are you serious?"

Kwan stopped his maneuvers with the toothpick. "About what?"

"That I'm bad for business?"

Kwan shrugged. "Ask her."

Ms. Tam blew smoke out her nose as she watched me walk toward her.

She asked, "How is Soo Jin?"

"She doesn't talk much."

"She never did," said Ms. Tam. "Even less, now."

"I guess she's all right. She brought dinner home tonight. She's sleeping now."

Ms. Tam stared at her half-empty bar. "People are scared."

"I've had a car following me, trying to intimidate me. An orange Jeep Rubicon."

"Doko family. One of the sons owns that car."

"They know where I live, where I work. I'm worried."

"The Doko know you were in my bar when they murdered Dae-Hyun. I think they wonder why you're not scared. Maybe they think you have plans of your own."

"Plus, I'm white."

Ms. Tam nodded. "You're white. They are gathering information about you. They're afraid you come from a powerful family."

I thought of my father sitting on his stained couch, watching cable news, a PB in his hand.

Ms. Tam smiled. "We know different."

"Indeed we do."

Ms. Tam's eyes went reflexively to Min Jee as she handled a customer's cash.

I waited until I had her attention and asked, "Can you help me out with something?"

"Maybe."

"I want to arrange a sit-down with the top guys in the Doko clan. I want to do it before they find out I'm a working-class grunt with no juice anywhere. Can you get a message to them?"

"What are you going to propose?"

"That we all get along, that we stop the bullshit. From what I've heard the Nang family is hanging on by a thread. The Doko won the game."

"This is a blood feud," said Ms. Tam. "There's no stopping. Maybe if you promise never to have sex with Soo Jin and to never give her a baby, maybe then they'll let you be. But why should they believe you?"

Something must have shown on my face because Ms. Tam said, "Oh. Too late."

"I think once was enough for both of us."

Ms. Tam said, "Maybe you'll fall in love with Soo Jin. Give her a blue-eyed baby boy."

"Can you set up this meeting?"

Ms. Tam reached behind the bar for a pen and a slip of paper. "Write your number on this. They'll call you if they want to talk."

I asked, "I got to wait on them?"

Ms. Tam didn't even bother answering me.

I walked back to the bathroom to take a piss before I walked home. When I was standing at the urinal the door pushed open. A tall Korean guy came in, dressed in a black shirt with a silver dragon over the pocket. He gave me a sidelong glance and then leaned over the small sink, staring into the mirror. I felt compelled to get out of the bathroom fast—I'd never seen this guy before—but I was in mid piss and committed to finish.

I kept an eye on the Korean. He did something which made me shake off and zip up—he reached under his shirt and placed a handgun on the sink. He leaned even closer to the sink and pulled his lips back, examining his purple-black gums.

The bathroom was small, and the Korean had to shift his stance to let me get to the door. Without making way, he looked at me and said in Korean what sounded like, "*Sonda bandagoo handle hand.*"

I frowned and said, "What?"

He tucked the gun back in his pants and moved away from the door to let me by, then said, "Don't try to cover the whole sky with the palm of your hand."

Ms. Tam was waiting outside the door. She pointed toward the kitchen and whispered, "Go out the back."

I slipped past the cook slicing vegetables and made my way toward the open door. I wasn't sure why Ms. Tam was looking out for me.

But I'd take all the help I could get.

FIFTEEN

The call came the next day, in midmorning, when Warsaw Wash was at its peak. I was surprised—the male voice on the line was young and soft, almost shy. The voice said they would meet with me at an office building on Wilshire. No way was I going to have a summit on their own turf. I told them that wouldn't work—that there was only one place I'd meet with them.

* * *

The concrete tables outside Ralphs supermarket on Western were a magnet for the neighborhood homeless. They could panhandle a few bucks at the sliding doors and then go inside and buy some fried chicken at the deli counter. I'd noticed no matter what their ethnicity, they always seemed to go for the fried chicken. More often than not, after their al fresco dining experience, they'd panhandle a few more bucks and buy some booze. They couldn't drink alcohol at the tables. They drank sprawled out on the grass on the south side of the building.

The meeting with the Dokos was set for three o'clock. I got there a half hour early so I could commandeer one of the tables. There were a couple of reasons I liked Ralphs as a location. Number one, it was public, and there were always a lot of people around. Number two, numerous buildings looked down on the tables, including a two-story parking structure. I could weave the fiction that I had eyes on us—armed men who would shoot if they saw me getting roughed up.

I sipped a Power-C Vitamin Water as I waited. Soo Jin had been even more quiet than usual when she was getting ready for work this morning. It was odd, having sex with her the night before and then being embarrassed to have her see me in my underwear. On the way out the door she had paused and then asked if I wanted dumplings again. I told her that would be good. I guess she got them cheap. Sooner or later I'd probably get sick of them, but for now they were fine. I'm guessing it made Soo Jin feel good to contribute in some way.

I looked at the time on my phone. 2:47.

A few minutes later a black Lincoln rolled into the lot, past the gatekeeper at the parking booth. For some reason—I'm not sure why—I knew this was the Doko clan. I watched the car pull into a handicapped parking space.

A young Korean guy in a black suit got out from behind the wheel and slipped around to the passenger-side door. He bent down and carefully extracted an old dude in a charcoal-gray suit. The suit hung on the old man's body like a scarecrow, as though he'd been measured for it when he was a heavier, more vital man.

The old dude looked straight at me, knowing who I was right off. The afternoon sunlight was bouncing off his waxed skull.

I stood up but remained close to the table. I didn't want a homeless guy swooping in and stealing our spot.

A third man got out of the car, tall and lanky for a Korean. He was dressed in a black suit, too.

All three walked toward me, taking their time. As they got closer, I recognized the tall Korean as being the same guy who tried to intimidate me last night in the bathroom at Ms. Tam's.

The old guy stopped in front of me and gave me the slightest of bows. I bowed back.

He slipped a silver case out of his suit pocket and thumbed it open. With both hands he offered me his business card. I took it and read: Shin Doko. That was it—no title, no phone number.

I said, "Sorry. I don't have a card. My name is Wes Norgaard."

"We know who you are," said Shin.

"Feel free to call me Wes."

Shin looked around. "You're alone?"

"I'm the only one who will be sitting down," I said. "But I'm not alone."

"We thought you would have more." He waved a dismissive hand at the youngest of the Koreans. "Wait in the car."

The tall Korean helped Shin sit down as the younger one headed back to the Lincoln.

Shin saw my look of confusion and said, "Four is an unlucky number."

I sat down across from Shin and the tall Korean.

Shin said, "You wouldn't come to us."

"No."

Shin frowned at the homeless at the tables surrounding us. "We would have privacy in my office."

"That's what I was afraid of," I said. "I saw what happened to Dae-Hyun in the Saja Room three nights ago."

The old man stuck his chin out. "And you're still fucking with us?"

Shin dropping the f-bomb surprised me.

I stared at the tall Korean and then back at Shin. "Like I said, I'm not alone. I own Warsaw Wash. My staff is Mexican. They're very loyal. Three of them are watching us right now. One of them did three tours in Iraq as a sniper. I don't want to hurt you guys, but I'm not going to be anybody's punching bag, either."

"It's not too late," said Shin.

"Not too late for what?"

"Annul the marriage."

"Soo Jin's been messed with enough," I said. "You should leave her alone."

"The Nang girl is damaged."

"Small wonder. You killed all five of her husbands."

The tall Korean smiled. "Perfect record."

I glanced up at the second level of the parking garage, as though I was making eye contact with my backup. I was hoping I didn't look too obvious.

"This is what I had in mind," I said. "Soo Jin and I will provide a banquet for the Doko family. You pick the place. It will be in honor of your family and a signal that the blood feud is finished. You go back to doing whatever you do—I'm sure you got better things to do than killing people—and we go back to a peaceful life of hard work and dumplings. How about it? Works for me."

"Why would we do that?" said Shin. "The Nang family is almost finished. This is a feud that has lasted three centuries. You think it will end because you honor us for a day?"

This wasn't going well. "I'm not going to annul the marriage," I said. "I thought maybe I show you some respect we can end this thing."

"You speak for the Nang family?" asked Shin.

"No. I don't even know them. The only one I met is Soo Jin."

"You offend their honor, making offers as though you were the head of the family."

I was getting sick of this old dude. "Where's the honor in terrorizing a girl?"

"I can smell you from here," said Shin. "It offends me."

"Jesus. You had to go there?" I knew the Koreans thought we stunk because of the dairy we ate.

The tall Korean pulled his suit jacket back—enough for me to see the butt of a handgun tucked in his pants.

I said, "What was that you told me last night, that I shouldn't block the sky with my hand. What'd you mean by that?"

The tall Korean said, "What's going on is bigger than you."

I said, "Don't even think of drawing that gun."

I stood up and backed away from the table. "You're an old man, Shin. Give this girl a break."

Shin got up slowly, the tall Korean bracing him by the elbow.

"We know you have nothing," said Shin. "A car wash staffed with brown monkeys. A one-room apartment. A shit car. No one is going to intervene on your behalf. I gave you reasonable terms. You have until tomorrow night to annul the marriage."

"Hey, old man," I said, slipping my hand around my back, as though I was carrying a gun. "Think the baby's gonna have blue eyes?"

SIXTEEN

I walked the two blocks back to Warsaw Wash looking over my shoulder, wondering if Shin was crazy enough to take me out in broad daylight. I wondered what it was like to have that kind of power. Commanding a stranger to annul a marriage. Telling a guy to sit in the car because four was an unlucky number. The old man could hardly stand up straight, but he still had plenty of swagger.

Maybe he was right—who was I to speak for the Nang family? Maybe they were sitting up nights planning how they could kill the Dokos.

I wondered how a family could carry a grudge for three centuries. In Pittsburgh it was more a live and let live, nobody's perfect world. People got in a rage and killed each other. If time got in the way, differences eventually faded away. People saw one another at baptisms, barbecues, corner bars—they had to get along. It was funny realizing Pittsburgh was more Zen than Busan.

Back at Warsaw Wash, the couple hours to closing I did paperwork, which I kept simple. I followed Jules's lead and paid my employees just enough to keep things legit. Instead of designating them as employees, I called them contracted labor, paying them a set amount and settling any overages in cash. Jules had kept all of the accounts in a ledger, with handwritten entries. Soon as my head cleared from my new investment, my new marriage, and the threats from the Doko family, I was going to buy an iPad and start doing all the record-keeping online.

I was standing on the sidewalk by the car wash, watching the last employee walk away for the day, when Yun pulled up. She opened the car door and said, "Get in."

I paused for a second and then realized I was in no hurry to get home and face Soo Jin. Last night's episode in the bedroom wasn't sitting well with me. I hadn't forced Soo Jin to have sex, but I'd been wondering if she'd wished she was somewhere else during the act, that she'd only been doing her duty. The thought made me embarrassed and angry. I could get that kind of loving at a massage parlor. It would also be a more honest exchange.

I got in next to Yun and she hit the gas. She lit up a Parliament and blew smoke out the window as she drove.

I looked at Yun's earthy, sensual profile. She had a small smile on her lips as she hung a left on Wilshire toward West Hollywood.

I asked, "You mind telling me where we're going?"

"One of my favorite places. The farmers' market over on Third. You ever been there?"

I thought about it and remembered I'd been there with Will, the first month we were in LA. We'd gotten drunk on pitchers of beer. All the way home I'd worried about being pulled over and getting a DUI.

"Not in a long time," I said.

"I'm taking you to dinner," said Yun, glancing my way. "I should have taken you three nights ago, before you got married."

"So you heard?"

"You're getting quite a rep in Koreatown. The Famous White Idiot."

"I had my reasons."

"I don't know if you're brave, stubborn, or stupid."

"Out of the three I'd probably go with stubborn."

We pulled into the lot. The farmers' market was a sprawling conglomeration of restaurants and shops, covered but open to the air. I followed Yun inside and wondered why I didn't come here more often. There was a relaxed vibe in the air. I was getting hungry walking by the stalls selling all kinds of ethnic food.

I asked, "Where are we going?"

"All the way down to the end, to the Cajun place."

The Koreans I knew were all Korean, all the time. They shopped, ate, and drank Korean. I was impressed and surprised by Yun coloring outside the lines.

I asked, "Are we celebrating something? I thought we did that yesterday."

"Maybe we are. Depends on you."

At the end of the corridor there were a bunch of tables in an open area surrounded by a handful of restaurants and a bar.

Yun said, "You order the beer. I'll get the food."

I'd never seen Yun outside the car wash. I only knew her as a customer. It was strange having her tell me to buy beer while she bought our dinner. I looked over my shoulder at Yun scanning the menu at a counter for a restaurant called The Gumbo Pot. As weird as it was being with Yun, it also felt good.

The bartender said, "What can I get you?"

I saw they had Sam Adams on tap and bought a pitcher. I sat down at a table and poured two glasses as Yun walked over with a loaded tray.

Yun set a plate of oysters on the half shell in the middle of the table, then two bowls of crawfish gumbo, collard greens, and an oyster po' boy. She sat down and took a long pull at her beer.

I looked at the spread of food. "Wow," I said. "We're off to a good start."

Yun compressed her lips together and then said, "My husband is dead."

I'd been reaching for an oyster and froze. "That's terrible. I'm really sorry for you. It sounded like you guys were married for a long time."

"I'm not sad," said Yun. "We were not man and wife for years. Tell you the truth, I don't think he even liked me."

I took a sip of beer, not knowing how to respond to this news.

"He died ten days ago, in Boulder," said Yun.

"Why didn't you tell me yesterday?"

"I thought I had more time."

I was thinking, *More time for what?* but I didn't say anything.

Yun went on with her story. "He went out to take care of his mother, thinking she was going to die of about a half dozen things that were wrong with her. She survived; he died. Of lung cancer. He never even told me he was sick. He smoked all the time when he was here. Maybe in Boulder, with nothing much to do, maybe he started smoking even more heavy."

"How are your kids taking it?"

"They cried at the funeral, but they'll get over it."

Yun reached for an oyster, doused it with lime and hot sauce, and slipped it down her throat in one gulp.

"He wasn't a bad man," said Yun. "But he had a cold heart."

I was about to say it was hard for me to understand her pain, because I'd never been married. Then I realized I was married.

"I should have come to see you ten days ago," said Yun. "Now, maybe it's too late."

"Are you in trouble?"

"No," said Yun. "I want to date you."

As the oysters disappeared one by one, Yun explained that she had wanted to hook up with me for a long time, but it just wasn't done in Korea. If a woman was married, she stayed faithful, no matter how lousy a guy the husband was. Koreans didn't get a divorce for minor reasons—like falling out of love. During the long march across a loveless landscape, the husband could screw around as much as he liked. The wife not at all.

Yun said, "For the rest of my life, I was expected to sit around wearing old-lady underwear and playing Chinese dominoes with a bunch of other miserable women. Now I don't have to."

I pushed a spent lime around on my plate. "If you had come to me a few days ago and told me this, I still would have married Soo Jin. I needed the money."

"I know you like me," said Yun. "You were just too shy to make a move."

"I'm kind of stuck here," I said. "Being with Soo Jin and all."

"I don't want a ring," said Yun. "I just want you to fuck me."

SEVENTEEN

I lay back in Yun's double bed, listening to the noises from the street. I felt wrung out—Yun had taken me through the paces.

I could hear her clanking around in the kitchen, making us a couple of mugs of green tea. On the way home from the farmers' market, Yun had called ahead and asked her babysitter to keep her kids for the evening. Once we got to her house—a one-story dilapidated Craftsman on Normandie—we didn't waste much time talking. We'd done it with her bent over the foot of the bed, with me on my back and her riding hard, and a third time more gentle and slow, face-to-face lying down on the bed, on sheets soaked with sweat.

I felt eyes on me and looked toward the door. A huge mastiff dog was sticking his head into the room, giving me the once-over. Yun brushed by the dog and closed the door.

"That's Jamjari," she said. "He won't hurt you. He can tell who my friends are."

"He's huge."

Yun handed me a mug of tea. She watched me take a sip and said, "I'm glad you're here."

The tea was strong. "You know," I said. "I went through quite a dry spell. Now it looks like I got more than I can handle."

Yun took my hand and put it on her breast. "I think you can manage."

I felt her nipple stiffen under my palm, and I pressed her breast. She moaned, and in seconds we were hip-deep into the fourth time that night.

* * *

Standing in Yun's living room as she looked for her purse, I took in the surroundings. The furniture was a mishmash of styles, probably secondhand stuff. A Mexican blanket—maybe a tapestry—covered one wall. It showed chestnut-colored horses galloping on a black background. I could see into the kitchen, where a refrigerator had photos of her kids held in place with magnets. A copy of *People* magazine lay on the coffee table. There was nothing in the house that screamed, "Korea."

Yun came into the room and switched on a light, still looking for her purse. I noticed an upholstered chair in the corner, with a wraithlike silhouette shadowing the wall behind, the shadow climbing to the ceiling like a dark ghost.

Yun noticed me looking and said, "That was my husband's favorite chair. He'd sit there for hours, smoking away like he was getting paid. Sometimes he wouldn't move or say anything all night."

"The shadow is from his cigarettes?"

"Black tar and nicotine," said Yun. "I'm gonna have to wash it off—it's too spooky. Like it's watching me."

Yun found her purse on the floor by the sofa. She took out her car keys and said, "Let's go."

* * *

I could have walked—it wasn't that far—but Yun insisted on driving me, since she had to go out and pick up her kids anyway.

The June night was warm. I put my arm out the window, cupping the air, feeling like a teenager again.

I said, "You didn't pick the greatest time to hook up with me."

"I had to grab the moment," said Yun.

"The thing I have with Soo Jin, it's a business arrangement."

"Are you going to tell her?"

"I want to see you again."

"Maybe you shouldn't tell anyone," said Yun. "It should be our secret for now."

The soft air felt fine. "That makes sense," I said. "People would think I was a real dog, marrying Soo Jin and taking up with you the same week."

We drove on in silence. I dug my wallet out of my pocket and said, "Let me pay for the extra time for the sitter. How much is she going to charge?"

Yun weighed this in her mind for a second or two. She pulled over in front of my apartment building. "Give me twenty. That should cover it."

I handed her a bill and said, "Am I going to see you tomorrow?"

Yun smiled, looked down. "I wish you were coming home with me tonight."

* * *

Upstairs, as I unlocked the door to my apartment, I heard voices. Then I realized it was coming from the DVD player.

Soo Jin was sitting on the edge of the bed, watching what I recognized as *Man on Fire*, a wild film with Denzel Washington wreaking havoc on a bunch of bad guys in Mexico City. I'd taken it out of the library a couple days ago. I must have watched it a half dozen times over the years.

Soo Jin looked over her shoulder at me and said, "I brought you dumplings."

"Thanks. Thanks a lot. I'll have them for breakfast."

The room felt really small. Maybe I wasn't feeling too proud of myself. I had no qualms about fucking Yun. But I should have called Soo Jin to tell her I wouldn't be home until late. Especially considering her track record with husbands.

Soo Jin stared at the TV as Denzel cut off a hood's fingers with a wire cutter.

I said, "Next time I'll call."

Soo Jin held out a scrap of paper in her hand. "My number."

Jesus. She must have been sitting there for hours, with that number in her hand, waiting to give it to me.

I took the number and saved it in my phone.

I asked, "You understand this movie?"

"Sure. The black man is trying to save the little white girl."

"I talked with Shin Doko today."

Soo Jin looked at me, eyebrows raised. She paused the film.

I said, "I tried to make peace with him, but he's stuck in his ways. The old dude knows you Nang are almost finished. He's not going to lay off. He can smell victory."

"I've never met Shin Doko," said Soo Jin. "But I know of him. Sometimes he sends me photos of all his grandchildren."

"What an asshole."

Soo Jin looked away. I made a mental note to watch my language with her.

"I got to ask you a question," I said. "What could have happened that was so bad that two families would fight for three hundred years?"

"It was a terrible thing," said Soo Jin.

"Is it too terrible to tell me?"

Soo Jin gave this some thought and then said, "There was a famine in the region surrounding Busan. People were dying. The northern part of the country was afraid the famine would spread, and they blocked the roads. Families held their food close, trying to survive. Bon-Hwa, a Nang merchant, gave Hyo Doko a short measure of rice—five hundred grams."

"Is that a lot?"

Soo Jin did the metric conversion in her head. "A little more than a pound."

"The Dokos and the Nangs are fighting over a pound of rice?"

"The Dokos are convinced people died because of that shortage. If it was just money or rice it could be repaid. But you can't bring back the people who died. The blood feud is all because of Bon-Hwa being greedy. Sometimes it makes me ashamed to be a Nang."

Soo Jin pushed play and went back to watching Denzel.

I opened the mini fridge and took out a can of Miller Lite. I popped it open and said, "Listen, there's something I didn't tell you."

Soo Jin sat a little straighter. "What's that?"

"I've got a disease."

EIGHTEEN

I didn't like the clinic, but I went there every week. I had to go. I had to give blood. Not that I was such a great guy. If I didn't give blood I would die.

I had hemochromatosis. Iron overload. If they didn't take blood from me every week or so my body would start to shut down. I'd lose my hair. Become impotent. Eventually I'd end up with liver cancer or cirrhosis. The doctors tried to sugarcoat things by referring to me as a "super donor."

Every seat in the clinic's waiting room was taken, and about ten people had to stand, either leaning against the wall or sneaking a smoke just outside the door. Most of those waiting were Mexican, although there was a sprinkling of elderly Koreans.

The clinic had plenty of reading material but hardly anything in English. I had to content myself with reading *Redbook*. I searched in vain for an even moderately interesting article and finally found one with tips on cutting your living expenses. Who would have known that you should keep your microwave unplugged when not in use—that a microwave can suck energy just sitting on the counter?

A woman with dyed black hair sat next to me. She looked to be in her fifties, a former beauty, dripping with costume jewelry and wearing a black slouch hat. I'd seen these types often enough, late at night in Ralphs. Hollywood driftwood.

Her eyes scanned the room and then fastened on me. When she turned my way I noticed a huge shiner under her right eye. She asked, "Can you spare some money so I can get some soup?"

I must have been a little slow on the uptake, because she said, "Not here. Later. At Friendly's."

I pulled out my wallet. "Yeah, I can spare a few bucks."

I dug out three dollars, and before I'd even handed them to her she was off on a rap: "You have gorgeous eyes—the prettiest I've seen in a long time. The eyes of a poet."

When she took the bills from me I saw how filthy her hands were. There was dirt worked into the creases of her skin and black grime under the broken nails.

She noticed me looking at her black eye. "You can see it?"

"Yeah. It looks like somebody hit you."

"My boyfriend—my former boyfriend."

She dipped into her purse for a bottle of makeup and started dabbing it over the shiner, saying, "This helps."

I told her, "Time will help."

The woman smiled with her lips pressed together. "Yes. Time heals all wounds."

I went back to my magazine, and the woman said, "You know, I had a very important career. I know very important people. I was a model and an actress. I had a part in *Basic Instinct*."

She waited for a second to let that bit of info sink in and then said, "With Sharon Stone and Michael Douglas."

I did some figuring. I was pretty sure *Basic Instinct* came out in the late '80s, early '90s. Twenty-five years ago.

"What part did you play?"

This question didn't sit well with her, and she said, "It doesn't matter."

The clerk at the intake window called the woman's name, and she moved quickly toward the door to the examination rooms.

It wasn't much longer until they called me. I walked down the hall, past the gurneys and the open doors of the waiting rooms, where I caught glimpses of nurses in burgundy scrubs and cheerless patients sitting slumped on exam tables.

I walked down to room six and sat down. The same guy treated me each week, and in seconds he came through the door. Royal Jones. My black nurse. I think the word in use was *thick* although most people would say Royal was fat. He wasn't a screaming homosexual, but even Cold War–era gaydar would tip you off quick that Royal wasn't daydreaming about women.

I remember the first time he took my blood and he had started in on one of his riffs: "When I was twenty-two years old I had a thirty-two-inch waist. I was a Royale. Now I'm a forty-four. I had the physique of a prince, and now I have the build of a pauper. A pauper who ate too much welfare cheese."

I liked him a lot.

"How are we feeling today?" asked Royal.

"You know how it gets around the end of the week." I said, "I start to run out of gas."

"Well, we'll set you up right."

He swabbed my skin and stuck the needle in my arm. I watched the blood go up the tube.

"You been eating right?" asked Royal. "You look a little peaked."

"Champagne and oysters, mostly."

Royal gave me a fist bump on the hand without the needle. "My man," he said. "You're learning how to enjoy life."

"When it rains it pours."

"Yeah, well, I wasn't going to say nothing, but I noticed that ring on your finger."

I glanced at the wedding ring on my left hand. "It's been a busy week. Got married and I bought the car wash on Western, where I work."

"Congratulations. I mean it," said Royal. "You got a picture of the lucky lady?"

I felt embarrassed—that was something I hadn't even thought of. "I'll have to catch you up on that next time."

Royal took the needle out of my arm and handed me a cotton ball to hold against the puncture mark.

"Someday. Someday soon I hope," he said. "I'll walk down the aisle."

This was a tough conversation.

"All you got to do is find the right guy," I said.

"At least it's legal now," said Royal. "My people are Democrats. But when it comes to homosexuals, black people are to the right of teabaggers. Same with the Latinos. They love all the social programs, but at their core, they're Catholic. They got the Catholic family values. No queers allowed."

Royal let out a sigh and sang a snatch of the Sister Sledge song. "We are family…"

He reached into a drawer and took out a plastic-wrapped chocolate chip cookie.

Royal handed it to me and said, "Here you go, Casper. Get that blood sugar up."

* * *

The rest of the day went by in a blur. During a lull in the action I drove out to Staples and bought an iPad, a scanner, and a download for QuickBooks. I spent the afternoon sipping a Big Gulp and setting up my new accounting system.

An hour before closing, a skinny white guy carrying a shopping bag showed up.

"You Wes?" he asked.

I told him I was.

"Here you go," he said, handing over the shopping bag. "Your shirts."

I looked in the bag as the white guy walked away. There were two dozen custom-printed T-shirts, with Warsaw Wash printed in blue. I'd asked them to make the capital Ws like drops of water—they'd done a good job.

I called the guys in and gave each of them two shirts. It was a small thing and didn't cost me all that much money, but it went a long way to making us feel like a team.

That evening I stayed in. I sat in my black vinyl chair as Soo Jin watched a Korean DVD I'd picked up from the library—a silly comedy. The English title was *My Sassy Girl*. Soo Jin seemed to be enjoying it.

Around nine Yun called but I didn't pick up. I needed a Fortress of Solitude night, even if my new wife was sitting across the room. Shin Doko's deadline to annul the marriage was only a couple of hours away. I wondered if there was still any hope of negotiating a truce, or if they were going to come at me charging hard.

I was almost done with the Colin Powell book, *On Leadership*. It was the right thing to be reading this week. I had a feeling some of his insights would come in handy.

Especially the one about being responsible sometimes means pissing people off.

NINETEEN

I was up early the next morning. A quick cup of instant coffee and I was out on the street. I liked being able to walk to work instead of battling traffic. The couple blocks of exercise was enough to get my motor running.

I was the first one at the car wash. I looked at the time on my phone—the guys should start showing up in a few minutes. I kept the chain across the entrance to discourage early birds and began preparing to open, unlocking and raising the sheet metal gate, flicking on the lights, checking the presoak. I'd done this a million times before, but the place was mine now; the feeling was different. When I washed the grime off at the end of the day, I was the owner, not some poor hump making bank for the boss.

I was standing inside the car wash when movement at the entrance caught my eye. I saw a guy step over the chain and walk toward me—a Korean guy. His hand swept under his jacket and came out with a gun. Still walking toward me, he fired, and I felt the bullet whizz by my ear.

I flicked a switch, putting the spray nozzles and the floppy wash arms into motion. Instantly there was a wall of water and flailing equipment. No way was he getting through there.

I heard two more shots—now he was firing blind. I took off, sprinting as fast as I could, keeping the building between me and the shooter. If he thought to hook around the building, he'd be on me in seconds.

I heard another shot, and the heel of my shoe went flying off.

I dug in and dashed across traffic, struggling to keep my balance with only one heel. I looked over my shoulder—no one was coming after me. I turned down another street, and then another. For all I knew the Korean was in his car and circling around looking for me. I thought to hide in the library, but it was closed. I kept running until I came to Wilshire and then hustled over to the line of cabs waiting for morning fares. I piled into the back seat of one and told the driver my address.

The driver looked back at me and said, "You know, you could walk that easy."

"I know. Humor me, OK?"

"Hey, it's your dollar."

In minutes I was unlocking the door to my apartment. Soo Jin came out of the bathroom wrapped in a towel, a second one wrapped around her hair. She didn't have to show up for work until ten. She asked, "Why are you here?"

I kicked off my shoes and dumped them in the trash. They were cheap loafers from Payless, not worth getting fixed.

"We thought I might be safe, being white?" I said. "Well I'm not. A Korean dude showed up at the car wash and started shooting at me."

Soo Jin's mouth opened in a tight O.

"I was alone," I said. "The other guys hadn't shown up yet. Shit, they're probably there now."

I dug my phone out of my pocket and called Manuel.

"Homes, what's going on?" asked Manuel. "I got here and the car wash was working all by itself."

"Are the police there?"

"No. What happened?"

"Anybody hanging around?"

"Just the crew, man."

"Look around. You see a Korean guy watching you?"

"We're in Koreatown," said Manuel. "There's a bunch of Korean dudes."

"I'm going to need you to dig deep. You want to be number two at Warsaw Wash, you're going to have to step up. Get the place opened and running and then come to my apartment."

"You in trouble, Wes?"

Manuel must have known the answer to that question: he'd never called me Wes before.

* * *

Manuel got to my apartment a half hour later. Soo Jin and I had already packed. I handed him my keys to the car wash and told him I was going to have to lie low. That some people had a problem with me, but it didn't have anything to do with the car wash, and no one was going to come after him and the guys. I gave him the account number for the bank and told him to pay the crew each day and bank the rest. Order supplies if we needed them and pay in cash. I'd call him later in the day.

Manuel had said, "You can depend on me, homes." He'd also given Soo Jin a favorable glance. It was clear he was thinking there was more to the story than I was telling him. But Manuel came from East LA, where you rarely heard the whole story, only bits and pieces, with the most important parts usually left out.

TWENTY

I drove my Dodge Dart around the block, with Soo Jin by my side and our suitcases in the back seat. I was careful not to drive directly by our apartment and instead circled warily around. Then I saw it—the Jeep Rubicon parked a block away. I hung a quick right and disappeared, putting distance between me and the Jeep. I looked in the rearview and was relieved when I didn't see it following me.

It was a full-court press, and I had only one player on the boards—me. I was going to have to find some allies.

I turned to Soo Jin, who looked sweet and unperturbed by all the morning's drama. "Honey, it's time I met the family."

* * *

I sat in a carved wooden chair made of some kind of tropical wood. I faced a sofa where three Koreans sat—an elderly woman, an old man, and an old, old Korean woman. What was left of the Nang family.

We were at what amounted to being Nang headquarters—a sprawling low-slung house on Magnolia Street at the outer edge of Koreatown. Unlike Ms. Tam's and Yun's homes, the décor could have come from an Asian prop house. The ornate furniture was heavily lacquered. A tall wooden screen with three partitions showed a scene of strangely painted clouds with golden dragons cavorting among them. A ceramic tea set was on the

MARK ROGERS

table, with tiny cups that couldn't have held more than a couple of mouthfuls of tea.

Soo Jin sat quietly by herself in the corner, her hands folded in her lap.

There was something peaceful about the room—but it was the peace of the dead.

The old man was named Kyu-Hook. The names of the women weren't offered, and it was clear that Kyu-Hook was going to be doing the talking for all of them.

"We are honored that you have taken Soo Jin as your wife," said Kyu-Hook. "Of course, we have spoken with Ms. Tam in detail, and we understand you entered into the marriage in full awareness of its unique exigencies."

"I was there when Dae-Hyun was killed."

"Then you are a brave man to have taken up our offer."

"No," I said. "It was an opportunity. I wasn't being brave."

Kyu-Hook smiled. "The Chinese character for *opportunity* and *crisis* is the same."

I'd heard that before. It seemed it was always trotted out when somebody wanted to give you a pep talk; a Chinese version of Vince Lombardi's "When the going gets tough, the tough get going."

"Well, this is a crisis for sure," I said. "That's why we're here. I met with Shin Doko two days ago and tried to convince him to deep-six the blood feud. He refused. Today he sent someone to gun me down. Luckily the only thing they hit was my shoe."

"It's fortunate that Shin was unsuccessful. But he will try again. He's been successful five times in the past with Soo Jin alone."

Kyu-Hook offered me some tea, and I held the tiny cup as he poured.

"From Seoul," said Kyu-Hook. "Mountain ginseng."

"I could use a boost." I took a sip. It was bitter and strong. I wished I had a quart to drink.

"The women of the Nang family are all past childbearing age," said Kyu-Hook. "What is left of the Nang family is in this room. Soo Jin is our only chance to keep the bloodline going."

I knew the Nang family was on the losing end of the feud, but I didn't know it was this bad. Only four left on the team and only one that could take the field.

I put the empty teacup back on the tray. "Can I ask you a personal question?"

"You can ask," said Kyu-Hook. "I'll decide if I answer you."

"What about you? Why don't you get a woman pregnant—hell, get ten women pregnant—and keep the Nang family going that way?"

"Twelve years ago I suffered an extraordinary experience with influenza. An unfortunate side effect was that I am now sterile." Kyu-Hook gestured to the elderly woman next to him. "Chun Hei is my daughter, and Soo Jin's mother. Chun Hei has suffered even more than Soo Jin."

I looked at Chun Hei. The suffering was written all over her face. Most Koreans were a lovely brown. Chun Hei's face was a sickly yellow. The skin sagged so much under her eyes I could have done it up with a safety pin.

"It is my desire to have a great-grandchild—a boy," said Kyu-Hook. "One that will keep the Nang family alive. Did Ms. Tam tell you?"

"Tell me what?"

Kyu-Hook glanced at the old, old woman and then said to me, "When you and Soo Jin have a baby, you will have to give it to us, to adopt and raise."

"No, Ms. Tam never told me that. It doesn't seem like a detail you'd gloss over in a business arrangement."

"It is necessary," said Kyu-Hook. "It is not a trick. In Korean culture, when Soo Jin married you, she left the family she was born into. She is no longer a Nang. She is part of your family. If you have a boy, you must give him to us to raise as a Nang. Only a boy can keep our bloodline going."

It took me a second to wrap my head around the concept. My mind had been so much on the business side of things—getting the down payment on the car wash—that I'd neglected the human side of the equation.

"Will I get to see the boy?"

"Of course," said Kyu-Hook. "He will be a Nang, but he will know you are his father."

Maybe it would be for the best, having someone else take over the responsibility of parenthood. I didn't feel like a husband, and being a father had never been part of my agenda. What kind of father would I be anyway? I'd been bought and paid for. Even my own dad hadn't sunk that low.

"As Soo Jin's husband, you are in great danger," said Kyu-Hook. "Your wedding vows have made you into a target. The Doko family is forbidden to kill the women of the Nang family, but they will stop at nothing to kill you."

There was a red lacquered box on the table in front of Kyu-Hook. He reached out and undid the clasp on the box. Inside was a stack of cash. The top note was a hundred-dollar bill.

"We will pay you to disappear with Soo Jin."

"How much money is inside that box?"

"Thirty-five thousand dollars. If a boy is born, there will be more."

It was tempting. Soo Jin and I would have to choose a place that had no ties to our past lives. That would be easy for me: eliminate Pittsburgh and LA and you had it covered. I'd heard good things about Portland. A big city like Chicago, we could probably get lost in. Maybe the key would be finding a city with hardly any Koreans.

Even as I ran these possibilities through my mind, I knew I was too stubborn to walk away from Warsaw Wash. I knew full well that I was never going to make the history books running a Koreatown car wash, but from an early age I never had a strong desire for the world's admiration. Making it on my own terms was good enough for me.

Anyway, once you start running, how do you stop?

I said, "Thanks for the offer, but hold on to your money. We're going to lie low for a while, but we're not running away."

Kyu-Hook closed the lid on the box. "This resource is here if you change your mind."

"We're going to have to find another place to stay."

Kyu-Hook nodded in agreement. "It's not safe in your apartment or even here. Shin Doko has men watching the house. In fact, he may already know you have come to see me."

That info didn't sit well. I stood up and said, "In that case, we have to move."

"Where will you go?"

"I don't know yet. I've never had a problem like this before. Up to now I've managed to slip in between the raindrops."

Kyu-Hook allowed himself a slight smile at this bit of whimsy. My mom used to say that to me all the time if she sensed I was avoiding responsibility.

Soo Jin came over to my side and said softly, "I'm late for work."

* * *

I dropped Soo Jin off in front of the Koreatown Plaza and told her I would pick her up at seven. I managed a quick drive past Warsaw Wash, and from the glimpse I got things seemed to be normal. I didn't dare stop.

I headed south on Western and took the ramp to the 10. I was glad to see that the traffic was light. Sometimes the 10 slowed to a crawl for seemingly no reason at all. Maybe LA itself was the reason.

I was at a loss—more confused than I'd ever been. I was a man of set habits. Work, home, supermarket, library, and the Saja Room. That was about it. I was an easy person to find if I kept to my routine.

Running to the police wasn't going to work. I hadn't done anything wrong, but I was certain they'd treat me like a criminal. There was no denying how unsavory it was marrying a woman for a cash payout. Also it was clear to me that the LA police had no clout when it came to a three-hundred-year-old blood feud. Maybe they'd make an arrest or two, but the Dokos would be swarming all over me as soon as the police looked the other way.

I wondered how I'd fare if things turned really tough. I wasn't tuned to violence—my last fistfight had been in junior high. I was in reasonably good shape, mainly because I ate well, I didn't have any addictions, and I was on my feet most of the day. I imagined what it would be like facing a martial-arts-trained Korean armed with nunchucks and shirikans. I didn't like where my imagination took me.

I was also clueless when it came to firing a gun. If you handed me a pistol I wouldn't know where the safety was.

I didn't feel up to the task of defending myself, but no one else was going to do it for me.

I swung down the exit for the 405 and headed south, toward Redondo Beach. I needed to talk to someone.

It might as well be Jules.

* * *

Redondo Beach was another world—far, far away from Koreatown, even though it was less than an hour drive. The air was clean and the ocean was blue. There was a feeling of prosperity in the air. Even the seagulls seemed relaxed.

Jules had been surprised to see me, although he welcomed me into his home. I got the impression my dropping in was a welcome diversion. He put a finger to his lips and motioned me to a chair. He disappeared upstairs and I heard low voices. When Jules offered to sell me Warsaw Wash, he had mentioned a problem with his wife. The way he was talking—the low, caring tones—made me think his wife was sick.

Jules came back down the stairs. "It's Mary. She's going to take a nap. Let's go out back and talk."

Jules's house was orderly. Everything was clean; the furniture was solid. Abstract paintings hung on the wall, swirling with colors. I stood in the kitchen as Jules poured us cups of coffee. I followed him out the back door to the patio.

We sat down, and Jules put a baby monitor on the table in front of him. He pulled a pack of Winstons out of his pocket. "Mind if I smoke?"

"No problem. It'll remind me of one of the places I can't go anymore—the Saja Room."

"You got eighty-sixed?"

"Not exactly."

I filled him in on what went down the last week or so. The arranged marriage, the blood feud, getting shot at. Jules hung on every word.

When I was done he said, "You made a big mistake. You're fucking with Koreatown. The only way to survive in that place is to keep to the railroad tracks. Wash their cars and go home to your white wife or your black wife or your Latina wife—but not your Korean wife. A white guy like you? You're not soluble in Korean culture. You won't mix."

"Did you ever have to negotiate with these people?"

Jules frowned. "Let me teach you a few things, if you don't mind. Never use the phrase 'these people.' It's like throwing a hand grenade into the conversation. I know you don't mean anything by it, but mistakes like that are gonna bite you in the ass."

"What would you do?"

"I wouldn't get into a mess like this in the first place."

"Yeah, but pretend you did. What would you do?"

"You're a good guy, Wes. You have a good heart. But if you don't mind me saying, you can be a little stupid sometimes."

Jules was old school, but calling someone stupid was *really* old school.

I said, "I came to you because I respect your opinion."

Jukes leaned back in his chair and took a deep drag on his cigarette, holding it in and then letting it out in an impressive plume of blue-gray smoke.

"You want to get out of the contract, no problem," said Jules. "I'll give you back your down payment, and I won't charge you a penalty. I'll even eat the attorney fees. I can turn around and sell Warsaw Wash tomorrow and make a better deal than I gave you."

"No. I want to keep Warsaw Wash."

"You made a lot of trouble for yourself in one week."

"Walking away isn't that simple. How many options does a guy like me have?"

"That's no excuse for being stu—"

"Hey!"

Jules's shoulders jumped, startled. He glanced at the baby monitor. "Keep your voice down. Mary's resting."

I leaned in closer. "Really, Jules. What should I do?"

"The smart thing to do is leave it all behind. Annul the marriage. Liquidate your assets. Find another job far away from Koreatown."

I thought about that—did the addition—and wasn't satisfied with the sum. I'd have my Dodge Dart. My nine grand in savings. A DVD player and a microwave. That was about it. My high school diploma would land me a job back in a car wash or a stock room. I'd be back to running a soapy rag over a car and vacuuming under the seats.

I wasn't a shining star. By dumb luck and staying in the same place for six years, I'd been handed an opportunity with Warsaw Wash.

I could walk away.

But I knew I wasn't going to.

TWENTY-ONE

On my way back to LA I stopped into an In-N-Out off the freeway. I realized I hadn't eaten all day—nothing more substantial than black coffee. I ordered and took my Double-Double and fries to one of the outside tables. Eating fast food was bad enough—eating at one of those plastic booths under the fluorescents gave me indigestion before the last French fry disappeared.

The June day was clear and warm. When I first arrived in LA I'd been amazed by the endless string of beautiful days. There seemed to be only slight variations in degree of sunshine and blueness of sky. I didn't miss Pittsburgh's winter slush or muggy summers.

My phone rang and I dug it out of my pocket.

Yun.

She got right into it. "Where have you been? I heard a rumor about what happened this morning. Is it true?"

"Things have gotten worse with this whole blood feud thing. I guess I thought I was bulletproof."

"Where are you now? I drove by the car wash and they told me you weren't there—that they weren't sure when you were coming back. Are you leaving LA?"

"No, I'm not leaving. But I have to figure something out. The Dokos are watching my apartment. I can't go back, at least not until I manage to negotiate something with Shin."

"I thought we had something."

This wasn't going well. "Yun, I feel fucking crazy. Like I've stepped into an alternate universe. I met with the Nang family today—what's left of them. They're finished. The Dokos have won."

"They don't think like that. When it comes to honor, for Koreans there's no gray area. Just black and white."

"Same with us Norwegians."

"I missed you last night," said Yun. "I called you."

"I couldn't talk to anybody. I don't think I said more than two words to Soo Jin, and she was in the same room."

"I felt jealous."

I felt like I didn't have time for this bullshit. But maybe that was my problem—why I spent so much time alone—I didn't make time for bullshit. "You don't have to be jealous."

"I was wondering if you were fucking her."

"C'mon, Yun."

"No, I was really jealous. My mind was playing all kinds of movies of you and Soo Jin. I had to stop myself from driving over there."

"What happened between us, that's real. With Soo Jin, it's all business."

"Then you haven't done it? You haven't fucked her?"

The lie came easily. "No, I haven't."

I could sense Yun's relief on the phone. "You said you can't go back to your apartment. Come here. Hide in my house."

"Are the Dokos going to mess with you?"

"We're not going to let them know you're here. And if they do find out, they won't hurt me."

"What about Soo Jin?"

There was a long pause on the phone, then Yun said, "Soo Jin can come, too. I have a guest room." Yun paused, then said, "You. You'll sleep in my bed."

* * *

The rest of the afternoon was a mad rush around LA, keeping my head down low while trying to do what I had to do. I withdrew a bunch of cash from the bank. Bought a half dozen biographies at a used bookstore. Called Manuel and was reassured that things were running well at the car wash. I'd seen enough crime shows to be paranoid about the Dokos somehow tracing our phones, so I stopped into Walmart and bought no-contract mobiles for me and Soo Jin.

I phoned Soo Jin and told her to call a cab when she finished work. She was to meet me at the jazz section in Amoeba Music—the room in the back. I told her not to tell anyone where she was meeting me. I then called Yun and told her to expect us when it was dark—that me and Soo Jin would make a dash into her house.

I found a garage for rent in Silver Lake and paid a couple months in advance to store my Dodge Dart out of sight.

We were going to ground, and I was going to do everything I could to make us hard to find.

It was almost seven thirty when Soo Jin found me in Amoeba, where I'd been reading John Coltrane liner notes for the last twenty minutes, all the while getting hairy looks from the staff.

Soo Jin looked even paler than usual, as though all the drama was bleeding the life out of her.

I asked her, "You took a cab?"

"Yes."

"You didn't tell anyone where you were going?"

"No."

"OK. Come with me."

I took her hand and led her through the store, by the rows of LA hipsters waiting in line to pay for their CDs and vintage LPs. We walked up the street a block, to the ArcLight. I'd been there a couple times before. It was a sleek movie theater, one of the best in LA. Soo Jin and I stood in the lobby, looking up at the electronic marquee showing movies and times. I picked the next film that was going to play, an action film out of France, with hopefully not too many subtitles. I bought us two tickets, and within minutes we were in our seats. Soo Jin had said she was hungry so I had got her some popcorn, Twizzlers, and a bottled water.

I had trouble keeping my mind on the movie, even though it was a barrage of gunshots, car crashes, and skullduggery. On any other night I would have enjoyed it. Tonight I was just killing time in the dark, until it was late enough to creep into Yun's house without anyone seeing us.

I leaned over toward Soo Jin's ear and said, "Today was your last day at work. You're going to have to quit the dumpling place."

Soo Jin stared at me, frowning. "Who will pay my bills?"

"Don't worry about that. Things took a heavy change today. Until I can sort things out, we're going to have to lie low. We're going to be living at a friend's house."

"How far away?"

"It's not like that. We're staying in Koreatown. It's just that we're going to have to hide from the Doko family."

"Who's your friend?"

"You'll like her. She's Korean."

On the screen, a Frenchman with a New York Yankees cap let go with both barrels, mowing down drug pushers left and right.

TWENTY-TWO

Soo Jin and I sat in the back of the cab as it shot down Normandie in the dark, heading toward Yun's house.

Soo Jin had been quiet most of the ride, until she asked, "What is her name?"

"The woman we're staying with?"

"Yes."

"Yun. I've known her a couple of years."

"Is she your girlfriend?"

Instead of answering Soo Jin's question, I said, "She was married up to a couple of weeks ago. Her husband just died. Lung cancer."

"Lots of Koreans die from that."

"Well, they smoke like chimneys. Us Norwegians die from suicide and the bottle."

"You don't drink that much."

"No. I've met Drunk Wes a few times. I decided I didn't like him much."

"Does Yun have a big apartment?"

"She's got a house. Not that big. Do you like kids?"

"Not really. They make me tired."

"Yun's got a couple of kids. And a big-ass dog—a mastiff."

"I like dogs. We used to have a little Maltese."

"This mastiff isn't going to be climbing into your lap."

The cab pulled over to the curb in front of Yun's address. I paid the fare and hustled Soo Jin up the walk to the front door.

We'd called ahead, and Yun had the door open before we'd made it up the steps.

As soon as we were inside Yun shut the door behind us. I noticed the shades were drawn, just as I'd asked.

I turned around and got a good look at Yun for the first time. She was wearing a short black dress with a plunging neckline. Her legs were bare and she wore black heels. Soo Jin's face didn't have a hint of makeup, while Yun had gone full bore with the eye shadow and lipstick. One looked like a woman; the other like a little girl.

Jamjari the mastiff was sitting in the corner, on a dog blanket by the sofa. He panted seeing me.

I waved a hand at the living room and said to Soo Jin, "Your new home."

Yun led Soo Jin to a chair. "Wes has told me about the trouble you're in."

Soo Jin said, "Thank you for helping us."

Yun's response was strange. I wasn't sure what she meant when she said to Soo Jin, "We can all help each other."

I went over to Jamjari and scratched him behind the ears. I asked Yun, "Are the kids asleep?"

Yun seemed distracted as she said, "You'll meet them in the morning."

Soo Jin yawned behind a tiny hand. Yun noticed and asked, "Are you tired?"

"Yes. Where do we sleep?"

"You'll sleep in the spare bedroom. Follow me."

I stayed where I was and looked down the hall as Yun showed Soo Jin to her room. When Yun walked back to me I saw Soo Jin in the doorway, catching my eye with a questioning look. Then the door slowly closed.

Yun said to me, "That girl is a drink of water. Me, I'm plum wine."

* * *

My hand trailed along Yun's full hip, down her thigh to her calf. Her skin was smooth. Heat was coming from her body, making the warm June night even warmer. When I leaned in to kiss her full lips there was a hint of garlic and something sweet on her breath.

I was already thinking of Yun's bedroom as a sanctuary. I loved how the moonlight and streetlights combined to give the room a pale illumination. There was a Bose stereo on the dresser, and Yun had put on a CD of Korean pop music to drown out any noise we might make. I had no idea what the singers were singing, but they all sounded like they were smiling as their hearts were breaking.

"No one can know we're here," I said. "These Doko idiots are crazy. They were gunning for me this morning, but any of those bullets they shot at me could have hit someone else. Some unlucky person walking by minding their own business."

"I won't tell anyone."

"I don't want you or your kids to get hurt by accident."

Yun trailed a finger across my chest. "You're gonna get even whiter, staying in the house all day. It'll make your blue eyes stick out even more."

I knew she meant to say "stand out," but I didn't correct her. Whenever I felt the urge to correct an immigrant's English I stopped myself—they knew twice as many languages as I did.

"Does your house have a fence in the backyard?"

"A big wood one."

"Maybe I can go outside if I wear a hat and shades, some kind of disguise. Does Jamjari like to chase a ball?"

"He's gonna love you if you play with him."

"Do me a favor? Be nice to Soo Jin. She's going to be confused by this new arrangement."

Something flickered behind Yun's eyes. "Does she think you belong to her?"

"I don't know what she thinks. I hardly know her. She's been through hell."

Yun said, "I have a feeling she'll be like a third child in the house."

I pulled Yun close. "I'll make sure everything runs all right."

* * *

The breakfast table was laid with empty plates and chopsticks. Across from me sat Yun's kids: her four-year-old daughter, Mi-Cha, and two-year-old boy, Tae-Yong. They'd looked at me warily when they saw me standing in the kitchen, mixing a cup of instant coffee. Yun had introduced me as Wes and told them in English that I'd be staying for a while.

When Soo Jin came out of the bedroom fully dressed, the kids stared at her.

Mi-Cha asked, "Are you a princess?"

Soo Jin smiled and took a seat at the table.

Yun said, "Soo Jin, help me in the kitchen."

Soo Jin got up dutifully. It was clear from the get-go that Yun was going to draw some clear lines in the sand.

I wasn't big on breakfast. Usually it was an egg on a hard roll, maybe a couple of doughnuts. I was bewildered as one platter after another came out of the kitchen: white rice, bowls of clear soup, pickled vegetables, a platter of smoked fish—still with their heads on. My nose was assaulted by a bowl of foul-smelling kimchi—fermented cabbage laden with red pepper. I took a sip of coffee to prepare myself for the onslaught on my belly.

Yun's T-shirts and shorts, her house with the Western décor and *People* magazine on the table—none of it had prepared me for this Korean breakfast spread.

Yun gave me a grin. "You were expecting Pop-Tarts?"

"You're talking to a Pittsburgh boy," I said. "Let's just say I'm more the drive-through type."

The kids attacked their rice like it was ice cream. Soo Jin picked up a small fish with her chopsticks and nibbled at its side.

I started with the soup, which was laden with bean sprouts.

"*Kongnamool gook*," said Yun.

"What?"

"*Kongnamool gook*," answered Yun. "That's the name of the soup."

I shook my head. "I am not going to call this stuff Gook Soup."

Yun laughed.

Even Soo Jin smiled.

TWENTY-THREE

I slowed down at the corner of Oxford and Seventh as Manuel trotted toward my rental, a navy-blue Ford Focus. I braked just long enough for him to get his ass in the seat, and then we were off again, driving toward Pico.

Manuel gave me a look that wrinkled his brow. "You sure you want to do this, homes?"

"I don't think I have a choice."

This morning I'd done an accounting. After making the down payment on Warsaw Wash, paying the rent on my apartment and the garage, and getting a rental car, I had about $5,500 to my name. If Manuel ran the car wash the way it should be run I'd do all right, definitely making my payroll and mortgage with cash to spare. I'd asked Soo Jin what she could contribute to the household, and she told me she had $800 in the bank. I told her we might not need it, but it was good to know it was there. I then sat down with Yun and told her I wanted to pay her mortgage while we were staying with her and that we'd make sure the fridge was filled. She tried to tell me that wouldn't be necessary, but no one drives double shifts in a gypsy cab for fun and games.

Then I called Manuel. At first he tried to talk me out of it, but he knew me well. He knew when I'd made up my mind.

"Let me do the talking," said Manuel.

"They're not going to try and jack me, are they?"

"Not with me making the introductions."

"How many cars came through this morning?"

Manuel ignored my question and asked, "You know any-thing about guns?"

"Nothing."

"My advice to you is keep it simple. A point-and-shoot handgun and a shotgun. You know, you could get a shotgun at Walmart for a much better deal than these dudes is gonna give you."

"If I use it, it's going to be pointed at someone. I don't want anything that can be traced back to me."

"I don't think they can do ballistics on a shotgun."

"It doesn't matter. I don't want to appear on a Walmart secu-rity tape running a shotgun through checkout.

"Whatever."

"I hope I never have to use it," I said. "But these Doko dudes are serious."

Manuel pointed ahead. "Take a left on Pico."

We drove a mile toward downtown when Manuel gestured toward a party store called Casa de Piñatas. I pulled into the lot and parked. A couple of windblown piñatas hung outside the door, and a bunch of birthday helium balloons strained against their strings.

I asked, "This is the place?"

"Don't believe what you see on TV," said Manuel. "We ain't going to a gangbanger's house with pit bulls and reggaeton, or some sleazy bar. This is where the action is."

I followed Manuel through the door. Inside were aisles stacked with tiny toys and pound bags of candy for piñatas. Mexican women roamed the aisles, trailed by kids. One side of the room had all kinds of paper plates and cups and table-cloths. The far wall stocked brooms and cleaning supplies for the after-party brushup. There was only one guy in the place, a hawk-nosed Mexican behind the register.

Manuel said, "*Hola*, amigo. How's it hanging?"

The hawk-nosed guy said, "I got your message." He looked at me and said, "I didn't know you were bringing someone with you."

"He's cool," said Manuel. "We go way back."

The hawk-nosed guy jerked his chin toward the rear of the store. "Go on back and see Noony."

I followed Manuel through a door in the rear wall that led to an empty room where there was another door. Manuel knocked on the second door and stood in front of the spy hole.

"Noony, it's me. Manuel."

The door opened, and we were waved in by a cholo with a shaved head, a carefully trimmed mustache, and a tattooed neck.

"Noony," said Manuel.

Noony said, "Yo, Manuel."

They exchanged a complicated fist bump and handshake.

Now I was squarely in cable TV/B movie land. Three other cholos sat on a shabby couch, giving me the eye. They were all dressed the same, in baggy shorts and white wifebeater tees. I was hoping Manuel had enough juice to float a gringo safely home.

Noony looked at me and said to Manuel, "This our client?"

"Yeah," said Manuel. "He's good people. Someone's been taking shots at him, and he needs to strap up."

Noony said, "You can vouch for the dude?"

"*Primo carnal*," answered Manuel.

Noony frowned. "*No manches.*"

"*La neta verdad*," said Manuel.

"Guys," I said. "I don't speak Spanish."

One of the cholos on the couch said, "*Bolillo, quiubo?*"

Manuel said, "He called you a white bun."

"Really?" I said. "Guys, let's dial it down."

Noony said, "All right then. What are you looking for?"

"Wes don't know shit about guns," said Manuel.

Noony walked over to a footlocker and flipped the lid. He reached in and took out a handgun. "We're gonna start you off with a ladies' gun," said Noony. "A .38 Special. Easy to load, easy to fire. Six hundred bills gets you the gun and a box of ammo."

I took the pistol and hefted it in my hand. "It's not loaded?"

Noony smiled. "No, homes."

I said, "I need a shotgun, too."

One of the cholos laughed and said, "Homes goin' to war."

Noony ignored him and asked, "Where you gonna be firing the rifle?"

"Home defense."

"Then you don't need to be more accurate than ten or twelve feet," said Noony. "A shotgun will do you. I recommend a sawed-off. It'll give you the option of chasin' around the city if you need to."

Noony opened a closet and pulled out a sawed-off shotgun. "This is a Remington 870. It's sawed down to twenty inches, so you don't have to worry about breaking the law. Anything under eighteen inches they gonna fuck you up. You got this one and a box of shells for eight hundred."

One of the cholos said, "You got that kind of cash, *gabacho*?"

Another cholo chimed in with, "Take his cash, homes. Keep the guns."

"I've got the cash," I said.

I got out my wallet and counted out $1,400 before they could change their minds or think of some way to jam a stick in my spokes.

I stuck the .38 in my belt, under my shirt. Jammed the boxes of shells in my pockets. I held the shotgun and asked, "You got a bag?"

When they were done laughing, Noony said, "You want a receipt, too?"

I slid the shotgun under my shirt and held it close to my chest.

Manuel asked, "You good with that?"

"I'm good."

Manuel turned away and said to the others, "We're gonna bounce." He repeated the same complicated handshake with Noony.

Then we were walking down an aisle of the store, with me gripping the shotgun close and hoping the pistol wouldn't slide down my pants, walking away under the watchful piñata eyes of Spiderman, SpongeBob, and the Little Mermaid.

TWENTY-FOUR

Back home, I locked Yun's bedroom door and laid the guns out on the bed. Manuel had brought me the iPad I'd bought for the car wash, and I logged in to Yun's Wi-Fi account and started in on my firearms education. I knew I wasn't going to have the luxury of training myself in the actual firing of the weapons, not unless I took a drive into the desert. Mainly, I wanted to know how to load quickly and where the safety was. After surfing the web for a half hour and watching a few tutorials on YouTube, I felt like I had a working knowledge in firearms safety and practice. I'd even picked up a few tips, like pointing the pistol like it was my hand and aiming and firing in a simple motion. I wasn't going to have to be a marksman—this was purely for protection if someone was bum-rushing the house.

There was a knock on the door. Soo Jin—she was the only one home.

I hollered out, "One minute." I put the guns and ammo on the top closet shelf, where the kids weren't likely to find them.

I opened the door.

Soo Jin had taken a shower, and her hair was glossy and wet. She was dressed in a white shift, and her feet were bare.

"There's something wrong with the TV," she said. "I can't make it work."

"Let me take a look."

I followed Soo Jin into the guest room, the first time I'd ventured inside. It was dismal. One side of the small room was stacked with cardboard boxes and plastic storage bins. A bed faced a chipped dresser where a bulky-looking TV squatted, playing noisy static. There'd been no attempt to decorate the room, and the walls were bare.

I picked up the remote on the bed, which was unmade from morning. "Why don't you watch TV in the living room? You're not a prisoner."

"I like it here," answered Soo Jin.

An answer like that is hard to argue with, and I said, "Well, that counts for something."

I pressed the settings button on the remote and scrolled through until I found channel 3. A Korean soap opera materialized in front of our eyes, some kind of drama with a baby-faced Korean dude waving around a bouquet of flowers.

I asked, "Is this it?"

"Yes," said Soo Jin.

After I showed her how to work the remote so it wouldn't happen again, Soo Jin settled into bed, her back propped up by two pillows, eyes glued to the set as though I wasn't there. Her knees were up, which gave me a clear view up her shift, to her white panties and the crease caused by the lips of her vulva. I took a few steps to the side, not liking the feeling of descending into Peeping Tom territory.

"With any luck, this won't be for long," I said.

Soo Jin looked up at me. "I hope we're here for a long time. Forever. I don't want you to die."

I stopped on my way to the door. "You think that's the only way out of this?"

"The Doko are strong," said Soo Jin. "And the Nang are weak."

Closing the door, I said, "I'm not Nang."

* * *

I watched Ms. Tam unwrap the present I'd brought her. She carefully took off the gift wrapping and folded it into a square. She held it up to me and said, "Good for later."

The gift wasn't much—just a box of Korean sweets—but I felt I should bring her something, since I was going to ask her for another favor.

I'd called Ms. Tam an hour ago, asking if I could come by her place before she left for the Saja Room. I'd been going stir crazy sitting around Yun's house. I had my own business at last, but I didn't dare go to it for fear of being gunned down. Before this mess, my life had a routine that would be boring to most people—but it was *my* routine. I liked being able to walk down the street, browse the bio shelf in the library, sing some karaoke in the evening.

Ms. Tam and I were sitting in the kitchen drinking aloe vera juice. Slimy pulp was suspended in the juice, and one sip was enough for me.

"I heard about your meeting with Shin," said Ms. Tam.

"It didn't go so well," I said. "They know they have the upper hand so they don't give a damn about negotiating a deal. Maybe I approached the whole thing wrong."

"You didn't show them the proper respect," said Ms. Tam. "We don't like doing our business in public."

"The tables outside Ralphs was a bad idea?"

"The word coming back to me was you shamed Shin, making him sit around with a bunch of homeless people."

I nodded in agreement. "I fucked up."

I could tell Ms. Tam thought I'd acted the ass. I tried to get her back on my side. "Did you hear they were shooting at me yesterday? A gunman ambushed me at the car wash."

"At first they were afraid of you. Because of your color. I think they did some digging and found out you were not powerful at all."

"That's true," I said. "On paper I'm not much."

Ms. Tam looked weary. I noticed mascara clumped on her eyelashes.

"I don't want to see you die, Wes," said Ms. Tam. "Don't go back to work. And stay away from the Saja Room."

"I'll stay away if it will make your life easier. But staying away from the Saja Room doesn't solve my problem."

"The Nang family has only a tiny bit of sand left in their hourglass. The Doko see this. They can taste their victory, and to them it's sweet."

"I never liked a bully," I said. "That's what this Shin is beginning to sound like."

"I'm sorry," said Ms. Tam. "I thought you'd be safe."

"What if I killed Shin?"

Ms. Tam made a face, like I'd just taken a crap on her kitchen table. "Don't talk like that. Don't even think like that. That would not be a solution."

"You know, Ms. Tam? I like to work. I like the simple things in life. Working makes me feel good. That's all I want to do. Pay my bills and go about my business."

"What are your dreams?"

"Keep it simple. Stay out of people's hair. Keep them out of mine."

"No bigger dreams?"

"I'd like a woman by my side. Someone I could really count on. Maybe one or two kids down the line."

Ms. Tam seemed to let this soak in. I figured it was a good moment to get down to business—get down to why I came here in the first place. "Do me a favor. Give me Shin's number."

Ms. Tam hesitated, then got up and rummaged around in a kitchen drawer, coming up with a pencil and a scrap of paper. She wrote the number down and handed it to me.

There was a worried look in her eye when she asked, "What are you going to do?"

TWENTY-FIVE

had it narrowed down to three places: Spago, Musso & Frank, or CUT. I'd spent an hour on my iPad searching for the proper restaurant to invite Shin Doko to dine on my dime. It had to be expensive, classy, maybe a little hip, but not too hip.

Yun brushed up against my back and looked over my shoulder at a photo of CUT. "That's a nice place. You gonna take me?"

Her jean-clad thighs felt warm against my back.

"Sure," I said. "Right after I get done romancing Shin Doko."

I clicked on the menu for CUT. They were serving Japanese Wagyu beef—$120 for six ounces. Plus it was owned by Wolfgang Puck, the guy on the pizza box. CUT it was. Shin was going to be impressed.

"You think he's gonna listen this time?" asked Yun. "A lot's happened since you had that first meeting. I mean, if that guy was a better shot you'd be dead."

"We're going to be in Beverly Hills, surrounded by people. He'd be suicidal to try to take me out in a fancy restaurant. Plus, Shin is in the driver's seat. He's not going to do anything stupid. I'm just hoping I can convince him that he's won. The Dokos are the champions. We've got one player on the field. Be a sport and call the game."

"I wish I could go with you."

"No way. I want to keep you out of this."

Soo Jin drifted out of her room and into the kitchen. She put a kettle of water on to boil.

"Make me a cup, too," said Yun. "Two sugars."

Yun asked me if I wanted a cup.

I shook my head no.

Soo Jin looked melancholy, and I asked, "What's wrong?"

"I think I miss my job," said Soo Jin. "I don't know what to do."

"It's not going to be like this forever," I said. "It can't be. We'd all go crazy."

"I know what you can do," said Yun. "Make some dumplings here."

The kettle whistled, and Soo Jin prepared the tea and sat down at the table with us.

Mi-Cha appeared in the doorway of the kid's room, dressed in Hello Kitty pajamas. She rubbed her eyes. "I can't go to sleep."

Yun said, "Lie down and close your eyes."

Mi-Cha said, "I can hear a doggy barking."

Yun waved her toward the kid's room. "Just lie down."

Soo Jin said to Yun, "Is it all right if I lie down with her?"

Yun looked like she was weighing the pros and cons before she said, "Sure."

Soo Jin got up. "I'll tell her a story."

Yun lit up a Parliament as we listened to the indistinct murmurs of Soo Jin's voice soothing Mi-Cha with a tale in Korean.

I said, "She's good with your kids."

"She thinks like a kid," said Yun.

I took the scrap of paper with Shin's number out of my wallet and reached for my phone.

"I still wish I could go with you," said Yun.

"Not this time."

* * *

CUT was all glass and light and polished metal. It was perfect. Shin Doko would never try and take me down here—it would be impossible to know if he was being watched. Any move on his part would be like getting violent onstage in front of a hundred people.

The phone call had been cordial enough, almost as though Shin considered the blood feud an entertaining sideshow. My proposal had been simple: be my guest at CUT so we can discuss an alternative to shooting up Koreatown. I could almost hear him nodding to his cohorts in satisfaction as the white boy finally showed him some respect. He agreed to the meet, and I asked him to keep the bodyguards to two—that I was on a budget. Maybe it was a Hail Mary pass, but I was prepared to spend a thousand bucks on dinner trying to soften up Shin.

I looked at the time on my phone. Where the fuck was he?

Then I saw him coming through the doors. Jules, looking all spruced up in a suit and tie.

The maître d' brought him over. He looked surprised when Jules insisted on sitting on my side of the table.

I said to the maître d', "We're waiting on some people."

Jules looked around. "I can't tell if you're doing me a favor, or I'm doing you one. I've heard about this place."

"Thanks for coming. I think we need a mediator."

"I don't know this Shin Doko guy, but I know plenty like him. You can't kiss ass and you can't step on toes. It's a delicate dance."

"I know how to skank and I'm good in a mosh pit. That's about it."

Jules gave me the once-over. "I don't think I ever saw you in a pressed shirt."

"I was lucky. It was still clean from my wedding last week."

Jules looked around the restaurant and gave me a corny thumbs-up. "Good choice. Those Koreans love the beef."

"You bring a gun?"

"Of course not," answered Jules. "Did you?"

"I'd rather not say."

"You know," said Jules. "I'm thinking of giving up my cable. You're better than TV."

I saw the tall Korean at the door, holding it open as Shin walked through. The maître d' brought them over and sat them. Cool that Shin brought only one bodyguard; the lighter the party the lighter the bill.

Shin had the regal thing going, as though he was the guest of honor. I realized I liked the tall Korean less each time I met him. He tried to pull off a sneering attitude, but he looked like the kind of guy who wore dirty underwear.

I decided to play it formal. "Mr. Shin Doko. Meet Mr. Jules Weinberg. Jules is a trusted friend of mine, and I thought he might help keep us on track."

A waiter appeared and martinis were ordered all around, except for the tall Korean—he requested a Coke. The menus were in front of us so we put in our orders for expensive cuts of beef.

I was surprised when Shin chose a rib eye from Nebraska. He must have noticed the look of surprise on my face. "Beef from Nebraska is the best," he said. "This is something to think about: what is most expensive is not always of the highest quality."

I had a feeling he was making an oblique reference to the situation I was in, but my wheels were spinning trying to figure out his "Confucius Says" comment. I'd already ordered the Wagyu, so I guess I lost that round.

"An astute observation, Mr. Doko," said Jules. "It could be applied to many things in life, from a pair of socks to the wife by your side."

"You understand," said Shin.

Jules decided to be a smartass and said, "I'm partial to Gold Toe myself."

I figured I'd try to make Shin smile. "Speaking of socks, we're running out of feet, Mr. Doko. We got off on the wrong foot the first time. I hope we can come to an understanding during this second meeting."

Shin didn't crack a smile. Instead he looked at me like I was a monkey.

I dug in and kept going. "A lot of people have died over this feud. I've met with the Nang family. They know they're beaten. In fact, I'd like to ask you a question."

"Go ahead and ask," said Shin.

"When was the last time a Nang killed a Doko?"

Shin gave it some thought and then said, "Seventy-two years."

I figured it had been a while, but that figure blew me away. Jules glanced at me with a look on his face that said, *This is some sick shit going down.*

"I did some research on blood feuds," I said. "I didn't know much about them. In no way am I trying to insult your honor, but I read that sometimes they can be settled with blood money."

"That's not our way," said Shin.

"If it was your way, how much would it take?"

"How much money would it take to turn back time?" asked Shin. "How much money to turn back time three hundred years?"

The waiter arrived with our meals. A wine steward brought over a red that Jules had ordered from the list. We were all quiet as we dug in.

But I could stay quiet for only so long. "You see," I said, "my proposal is we pay the Doko family blood money. I was thinking fifty thousand. If it's a matter of pride, maybe you could give it to a Koreatown charity or something. That way, something good could come out of putting this thing to rest."

"A boiling pot on the stove does not rest," replied Shin.

"Sure it does," I said. "You just have to turn the heat down."

"Wes is making sense, Mr. Doko," said Jules. "Also, let's face it. You kill a white guy and you're gonna bring a shit storm down on your head. They'll turn Koreatown inside out."

Shin held his glass of red in front of him. "Your friend has made his own trouble."

"Killing Wes is bad for business," said Jules. "You're not dumb. Figure it out."

I kicked Jules's leg under the table; he gave me a look like he was going to slap me.

"This ain't Korea," said Jules, wagging a finger at Shin. "This is LA. The U...S...of A. You wanna make money hand over fist, go at it. But don't go around shooting people."

Shin glanced down at his plate as though he'd lost his appetite. The tall Korean was shifting in his seat like he wanted to throw down on Jules.

"Jules," I said. "Cool it."

"No," said Jules. "This guy talks like he's figuring to shoot you down like a dog in the street."

Shin took a sip of his martini and said to Jules, "Your friend Wes is not a dog. He is a male whore. He sold his virtue for money."

I had no problem being called a whore, but it didn't sit well with Jules. "You want a blood feud?" he said. "You ever hear of the Weinbergs? Check out the LA phonebook. There's thousands of us. You want to wipe us out, you're gonna have to go nuclear."

I tried to restore some order and said, "Can we get back to this charity idea of mine?"

* * *

After leaving the restaurant we waited outside the door until we saw Shin Doko being driven off in his black Lincoln. I didn't want them to see my rental, the blue Ford Focus.

I walked Jules over to the parking garage across the street, where we both had parked.

"Don't even say it," said Jules, walking two steps in front of me. "The cocksucker had it coming."

"You were supposed to be a mediator."

Jules was fuming. "I am so glad I am in Redondo Beach, where I don't have to deal with these arrogant motherfuckers anymore."

The parking garage had a hundred dark corners where a person could hide. Our footsteps echoed as we walked. The combination was making me jumpy.

Jules took out his keys and beeped his car unlocked. I watched him get behind the wheel and power down the window.

I put my hand on the open window of the car. "They're not going to negotiate, are they?"

"Not a chance," said Jules. "They're dug in. They were dug in before the meeting. You took your shot. My advice to you? Don't expect any wiggle room with this Shin Doko character."

Jules keyed his ignition, and the Grand Marquis's engine roared loudly in the cavernous space.

"Wes," said Jules. "Think hard about walking away and cutting your losses. Hanging tough is well and good, but these guys lack imagination. They're going to try and kill you."

"I'll think about it."

"Don't waste too much time thinking."

"I'll let you know what I'm going to do."

Jules said, "Watch your back."

Then his car was heading toward the exit.

TWENTY-SIX

I handed over a twenty to the parking lot attendant, and she asked me for three more dollars. I kicked myself for not having my parking stub validated at CUT—I'd been too angry over Jules making a mess of things. Talking with Shin should have been like settling slowly into a hot bath, all of us getting warm, scrubbing one another's backs, seeing eye to eye. Instead, Jules had flipped us ass over elbow into boiling water. He liked calling people dumb, but it was Jules who was the dumb one today.

I pulled into Wilshire and headed north toward Koreatown. It was the tail end of rush hour, and the traffic carried a burst of nervous energy, of people trying to get home or to an evening meeting. This part of LA always made me think of Hollywood. Maybe it was the billboards advertising movies, the occasional Bentley, the blondes with fake tits and big scripts. I thought how distant Koreatown was from all of this. We were so far removed from the Dream Factory we could have been in Duluth. I was glad. I liked a good movie, but I didn't need to have Hollywood shoved in my face 24/7. Washing cars was an honest living. It was nothing to be ashamed of. Maybe I experienced the odd moment or two when I thought I could be doing something more important, but those dreams of glory soon passed. When I was thinking clearly, I was glad I was right where I was.

Pulling up to a traffic light, I looked reflexively in my rearview mirror. There it was—that hideous orange Jeep Rubicon. An old joke blew into my mind: he thinks he's a wit but he's only half right. I'd been careful making sure Shin was gone before I drove off, but not careful enough to make sure he hadn't posted a second car to tail me. I was new to this; if they ever chose to follow me in something other than an orange Jeep, I was a goner.

I hung a left on Santa Monica and the Jeep followed. An equation occurred to me: Lose Jeep + ditch Focus + find mass transit = saving my ass.

When you work six years in a car wash, you tend to evaluate every outfit you drive past. I knew the Elephant Car Wash on Santa Monica entered on Santa Monica and then spit cars out onto Hilldale. Three blocks later I saw the silly sign with the baby-blue elephant splashing water on a convertible full of laughing passengers. I hung a left and took my place in line.

An attendant rushed over to the driver's side of my car. "Plan A, B, or C, sir?"

I looked at the board and saw that Plan C was the cheapest—just a simple wash, no undercarriage stuff or hot wax protection. I handed the attendant twelve bucks and said, "Give me C."

I rolled up closer to the entrance of the car wash. So far, so good. No one was behind me. I looked in my mirror and saw the Jeep idling at the entrance of the car wash. This was LA—where the flow of traffic ruled. They were going to have to make a decision quick which way they were going to jump.

I saw the Jeep drive away. Without a doubt they were going to circle the block and pick me up at the exit.

I jammed it into reverse just as a heavy-duty Tacoma was pulling into the lot. Luckily the driver was timid enough to hit the brakes to give me room to back out of the car wash lane. I fishtailed in reverse into the middle of Santa Monica, praying I wouldn't get tail-ended. I straightened and then shot into traffic. Instead of heading toward Koreatown, I blasted down Santa Monica toward the 101 freeway exit. I'd pick up the 405 south and then bomb down to long-term airport parking at LAX. I'd ditch the Focus and take a bus back to the city and a cab home to Yun's.

I was done playing around.

It was time to come out of the cold.

TWENTY-SEVEN

The Olympic Division police station on Vermont resembled a run-of-the-mill grammar school building; three stories of brown brick and glass. I parked my new rental at an empty meter across the street and took a deep breath.

Last night it had taken me a couple of hours to get home to Yun's after leaving my Ford Focus at the airport. This morning Yun caught a fare to LAX, and I rode shotgun. I picked up the Focus in long-term parking and drove it back to the car rental agency in Silver Lake, exchanging it for a green Jeep Cherokee. Hopefully I wouldn't get made so quickly this time.

So far my luck had been good, ducking bullets and dodging the tail. But I knew my luck couldn't hold forever. The stakes were too high if I did slip up. Shin had made it clear he wasn't going to negotiate with me. If I brought the police into this and they managed to shine a light on Shin, he might have to cut his losses instead of being such a sore winner.

I had a sick feeling in my stomach as I entered the lobby of the police station. I hated anything to do with the courts, or the police or the IRS—I hated placing myself in their power. I couldn't shake the feeling that it could always go two ways with them—they could prop me up or bash me down. I was subject to their whims. A cop could have a fight with his wife at the breakfast table, and he'd take it out on me. An IRS agent might get told he's not posting the right numbers and put me under the microscope. I stayed as far away as possible from all authority.

I asked a cop where to go to file a complaint, and he pointed toward a Plexiglas wall with teller windows, similar to what you'd see in a bank.

I walked over. My heart sank when I saw the sole police officer behind the glass—a Korean with a shock of black hair.

I leaned in and said, "I may have to kill somebody. I'd like to register a complaint so I'm on record that my life has been threatened."

The Korean officer didn't make a move to write anything down. He didn't even ask me for identification. Instead he said, "Can you explain the situation you find yourself in?"

"I've angered a Korean family, and I'm caught up in the middle of a blood feud."

"What did you do to anger them?"

I didn't like where this was going. I didn't want to tell him I was paid twenty-five thousand to marry a Korean woman. Technically it wasn't against the law, since Soo Jin was a citizen. But it would make me look like a sleaze. I had the fleeting, disheartening thought that maybe I was.

"I'm not really sure what I did," I said. "But they threatened me."

"Did you threaten them back?"

I thought about that for a moment. "Yeah, I guess I did."

"Then you're caught in a bind," said the Korean officer. "Since this person could make a counter complaint. You could both be charged with making terroristic threats."

"But he took a shot at me."

The cop looked confused and asked, "The man who made the threat?"

"No," I said. "Another Korean dude."

"Could you identify the shooter?"

"No, not really," I said. "He was Korean. A Korean dude. Black hair. Not so big."

I realized my description wasn't sitting too well with the Korean officer taking my complaint. He asked, "Were there any other witnesses to the shooting?"

"I don't think so."

"When did it happen?"

"A couple of days ago."

"Why didn't you make a formal complaint when it happened?" His face wore an unsympathetic expression. It was clear he was restraining himself from asking the question that was really on his mind: What are you trying to hide?

I said, "I guess I was in shock."

"Who is it that made the threat against you? You said it was a Korean family."

I hesitated. "Yeah, well…"

There were three people in line behind me. The Korean officer slid a form through the slit in the Plexiglas.

"Fill this out and bring it back to me. It's a formal complaint."

"What's going to happen after that?"

"If anything else happens, you'll be on file as having made a complaint."

"Can I get police protection?"

A white cop might have laughed; the Korean cop looked at me with a blank expression on his face as he said, "No."

"And if I kill somebody in self-defense?"

The cop frowned. "You're treading a fine line. More talk of that nature and you risk being detained for your own safety and the safety of others."

"You got a pen?"

He handed me a stubbly little pencil, and I made my way over to a line of plastic chairs. I started filling in the form, giving them my home address and the address of Warsaw Wash. I came to the section where I was supposed to describe what had happened to me. I made a few halfhearted marks with my pencil before I gave up.

Who was I kidding? I was making a complaint against a powerful man. I was delivering my fate over to those who held the power. They'd all have a laugh as they squashed me like a bug.

I folded the paper into a small square and put it in my pocket.

A few minutes in the halls of power and I didn't even trust the sanctity of the wastebaskets.

* * *

Yun's house was peaceful in the afternoon, even though my insides were churning. I rummaged through her cabinets and found a can of Chunky Sirloin Burger soup. I could hear Soo Jin's TV going in her room—a lot of Korean chatter over frequent applause.

I walked over and knocked on her door. She must have hit the mute because the noise of the TV stopped. She opened the door, which released a puff of stale air. Soo Jin looked sleepy, even though it was one in the afternoon.

"You want some soup?"

She gave me one of her wan smiles and walked over to the kitchen table. I dished out the soup and brought the two bowls over to the table.

Soo Jin said, "I heard you go out this morning? Where did you go?"

"I switched rental cars and then did what I thought was the right thing—I went to the police station."

Soo Jin looked down at her bowl. Even she knew that had been a stupid move.

"I didn't tell them anything," I said. "I walked out without giving them names or why I was there. We're going to have to solve this ourselves."

"It's good you walked away," said Soo Jin. She made a ball of fingers with her clasped hands. "The Doko and the police are like this."

Chunky Soup was strange. I'd been eating it all my life, and I still couldn't tell you if it was good or lousy.

I looked up at Soo Jin. She looked miserable.

"You're like all the others," said Soo Jin.

"How?"

"All my life," said Soo Jin. "Even when I was a little girl, they would look at me and be sad. They knew any man that chose me would be in danger."

"Did you ever love any of these guys?"

"That would be even worse. I think I prepared my mind and heart not to fall in love."

I felt sorry for her, imagining a teenage girl afraid to fall in love, knowing it would be a death sentence for the guy who took her hand in marriage. I guess it was like convincing a bird it couldn't fly; sooner or later its wings would be useless.

I decided to change the topic. "What do you do for fun, anyway?"

"I like to shop. I watch my shows on TV. Sometimes I go for ice cream."

"Oh yeah? What's your favorite?"

"Red bean."

"That's a flavor?"

"That and green tea ice cream."

"Well, maybe we're going to have a party tonight. When it gets dark I'll shoot out and get us all some ice cream. I'm partial to butter pecan, myself. You ever sing?"

"You mean karaoke?"

"Yeah. You sing karaoke?"

"The night with Ms. Tam at the Saja Room was the first time I was in a karaoke bar. Good girls don't go to bars."

"That's an old-fashioned way to look at it."

"I sang karaoke at a party. Mostly Korean songs."

"You know any songs in English?"

"Sugar Sugar."

"Maybe we could do a duet sometime."

Soo Jin smiled.

"You know what?" I said. "I have a couple of ideas. If we're going to be stuck in this house, we got to get you out of that room. It's not healthy. We all have to start doing stuff together, instead of living like we were a bunch of strangers. We'll start tonight with ice cream and a movie. I'll pick something the kids can watch."

My cell rang. Yun. I picked up and said, "Hey, babe. What's up?"

I saw Soo Jin wince at hearing me call Yun "babe."

Yun sounded stressed. "I just got a call from my babysitter. She's got some kind of family emergency, and she needs me to pick up the kids. I'm all the way down at Long Beach. I'm waiting on a fare down here. Plus, rush-hour traffic is going to be twisted."

I'd noticed that Yun sometimes used weird slang with overtones of the '80s. Probably stuff she'd picked up from Hollywood movies.

I asked, "You need some help?"

"Can you pick up the kids? Maybe you can wear a disguise or something."

"Sure. I'll pick them up. Give me the address."

I wrote the address down—it was only a dozen blocks away.

Yun said, in low tones, "I owe you one…I think I'm falling in love with you."

"This is definitely my year." I couldn't help laughing into the phone. "If I can only survive."

I grabbed the car keys and said to Soo Jin, "Be back in a few. I have to pick up the kids."

"Do you want me to come?"

"That's not a good idea. We stand out too much together. We're the Brangelina of Koreatown."

I looked around for a disguise of some sort. I found a Dodgers baseball cap of Yun's and some huge shades. It wasn't much, but it was better than nothing.

* * *

I drove down Mariposa looking for the address. Yun had told me it was a small Mexican-style house with a red tile roof. I saw it right off—it stood out on a block of drab wooden houses. I found a parking space half a block away and walked up to the door. The sitter—a middle-aged Korean woman—must have been watching from the window. She had the front door open before I made it halfway up her walk. I felt exposed and hunched my shoulders. I wanted to do this quick and get out of here.

Mi-Cha and Tae-Yong came through the door, looking cute and well-scrubbed.

"Where's Mommy?" asked Mi-Cha.

"She's out there working hard," I said. "You get to ride with me today."

The Korean woman gave me a half bow and said, "Thank you."

"It's not a problem. Hope your emergency works out."

The Korean woman bowed again and disappeared inside.

I took Tae-Yong by the hand. Mi-Cha walked by my side.

Just to make conversation, I asked, "What did you guys do today?"

Mi-Cha said, "Ate papaya."

"Oh, yeah?"

"And we got to watch one show," said Mi-Cha.

"Oh, yeah, what was that?"

That's when I felt the blow against the side of my head. I let go of Tae-Yong's hand as I fell against a wrought-iron fence. The second punch hit me in the kidney. I swung my head around to see my attackers and got slammed in the jaw. There were at least two of them.

Mi-Cha screamed.

The fence was the only thing keeping me up. I gripped it with both hands as another punch rocked into my kidney. I pushed back and whirled around and saw my attackers—two young Korean guys. I glanced at Mi-Cha as they moved in on me—she was holding on to her brother, tears streaming down both their faces. I moved to my right, trying to put some distance between me and the kids.

The two Koreans came in together—they were good at this. I got my fists up and got a kick in my thigh for my trouble. My leg went numb. They moved in and went to work, taking me apart. As I hit the ground I had the comforting thought: if they were going to kill me, they would have shot me.

If I was in a boxing ring the ref would have stopped the fight. Instead it went a few beats too long—literally. When they were done I was huddled on the sidewalk, my cheek pressed against the grit, watching them walk away, turning the corner. They were smart not parking on the same street. It didn't matter all that much. No way was I going to chase them.

I looked back at the babysitter's house. I thought I saw a curtain move, but I wasn't sure. I wondered if she'd set me up.

Mi-Cha tugged on my sleeve. "Wes…Wes…"

I got up to a sitting position. There were sharp pains darting through my torso. I touched my face and felt blood at the corner of my mouth.

When I stood up I could feel my left leg was still numb. But I figured I could make it to the car.

Tae-Yong was bawling.

Mi-Cha said, "I want Mommy."

"Kids," I said. "Don't be afraid. No one's going to hurt you. We're going home."

I hugged Tae-Yong with one arm. "Everything's going to be OK."

The boy let out a few deep sobs and calmed down a bit.

"Mi-Cha," I said. "Take your brother's hand. We have to walk down to that green car."

My disguise had been knocked from my head into the gutter.

I pointed and said to Mi-Cha, "Hand me the hat and sunglasses—they belong to your mom."

She snatched them up and gave them to me. I kept one hand on the wrought-iron fence and hobbled alongside the kids, heading toward the Jeep Cherokee.

Then I saw them coming back.

It took them half the effort this time, putting me down on the ground. Maybe I even passed out for a few seconds. A kick to the head was the worst of it.

When I got off the cement, weaving on my knees, the kids had stopped crying. Mi-Cha pointed at my face, looking scared to hell.

My hand went to my brow and came away awash in blood.

TWENTY-EIGHT

Green tea ice cream wasn't half-bad. There was a grit to it that reminded me of the sidewalk against my cheek.

I sat propped up on the couch, watching a Disney film, something about a redheaded Scottish girl called *Brave*. I could hardly keep my mind on it, but the kids and Soo Jin seemed to be enjoying themselves.

Yun sat next to me, looking worried every time she glanced at my face. I had a purple bruise on my jaw, and I was black and blue over both kidneys. The cut had been along my hairline, and while the blood had flowed plenty, it was really no more than a scrape. The inside of my mouth was torn up, which is probably why the green tea ice cream tasted so good.

When I'd gotten home and the kids had been reassured that the sky wasn't falling, I'd raided Yun's medicine cabinet and doubled down on extra-strength Excedrin. The pain was now just a whisper.

The Dokos had sent a message. Even though no words were exchanged, it was easy to figure out what they were saying. We'll fuck you up, and then we'll fuck you up—until you back away from Soo Jin and go about your business.

One thought kept bothering me.

I asked Yun, "How well do you know your babysitter?"

"Just a little. Why?"

"The beating I took went down too smooth. I don't think Navy SEALs could have executed it any better."

"What are you trying to say?"

"I think I was set up..."

"She wouldn't do that."

"What's her last name?"

"It's not Doko."

"I feel like going over there and shaking the truth out of her."

"That would be stupid. If she did set you up and she tells you, what are you going to do? You can't go to the police. You already know it's the crazy Doko family making your life miserable. So what are you gonna do? Beat up an old lady?"

"She's not that old."

Yun laughed. "Motherfucker..."

"Why did these assholes shoot at me one day and beat me up the next? It doesn't make sense."

"This whole thing is crazy," replied Yun. "Blood feuds are crazy. It's fuckin' medieval. It's enough to make me wish I wasn't Korean."

"Do you think those two who kicked my ass will put two and two together and figure I'm living here with you? Why else would I be picking up your kids?"

"I think it was just bad luck that those guys saw you. I was wrong to ask you to pick up the kids."

"You weren't wrong. I go crazy doing nothing all day. I was glad I could help."

"I'm not going to ask you again."

"Do me a favor. We should have thought of this before. Fire the babysitter. Keep the kids home. Soo Jin can take care of them."

Yun turned this over in her mind. "It will save me some money."

I said, "Soo Jin."

She turned around, still smiling at what she was watching on TV.

"Do you mind taking care of the kids?"

"When?"

"Every day."

Soo Jin said, "I don't mind." She turned back to the show.

It occurred to me that this blood feud had stunted Soo Jin's development. Maybe a part of Soo Jin's mind didn't want to admit she was a grown woman. I couldn't blame her, really. Passing through puberty and coming out the other side had meant a string of suitors getting whacked. It was enough to make anyone regress into a childhood trance of ice cream and cartoons.

I stared at the TV screen, where Scottish lords in kilts were knocking each other around like they were the Three Stooges.

Mi-Cha poked Tae-Yong in the shoulder with a finger.

Tae-Yong reached out and laid a clumsy slap on the side of Mi-Cha's face.

* * *

Yun was fast asleep, her hand flung back over her head, her right nipple pointing at the ceiling. It was way past midnight and I still couldn't sleep. Maybe it was a delayed reaction, but I felt close to tears, thinking of the beating I'd taken. I was angry, too—but mostly I felt a sense of shame. They had kicked my ass. I hadn't backed down, I hadn't begged for mercy, but I also hadn't landed a punch. If I'd had my gun with me, I wondered if I would have used it. A film loop kept playing in my head, of me drawing my pistol—seeing the surprised looks on the Korean dudes' faces—and then blowing them backward into the street.

Also, with the house quiet and everyone sleeping, a thought kept tunneling into my brain: if the babysitter is in on this, then she knows I'm connected with Yun in some way, since I picked up her kids. What's stopping them from bursting through the door? They'd tried shooting me, they'd beaten me—what's next: torture? These were the kind of night thoughts that made me sweat into the pillow with my eyes wide open.

I got up and padded into the kitchen, dressed in boxers and a white T-shirt. I prepared a bowl of cornflakes with bananas sliced into it and sat at the kitchen table in the dark. I ate the cornflakes, thinking I had no one to blame but myself. All things come to he who waits. Well, I hadn't waited—I'd pushed myself to the front of the line. I'd gotten my car wash and a whole lot more I hadn't asked for. I'd been greedy and I'd been stubborn.

I'd talked to Manuel earlier. Warsaw Wash was humming along. There were no suspicious characters lurking about. Manuel told me he'd been paying the crew, ordering supplies, and making daily deposits in the bank. He'd joked that I should go to Hawaii or something, that he had everything under control. What Manuel didn't realize was that I liked working. I liked marking my day with nine hours of toil topped with some hard-earned leisure.

I had an idea. I looked at the clock: it was almost three. I'd have to wait until at least eight o'clock in the morning before I made the call.

I put the bowl in the sink and ran some water over it. Heading back to bed, I hoped I could put a few hours between me and the morning.

* * *

Eight o'clock found me standing in the kitchen with my cell phone in my hand. I'd been up since six, taking a shower, tidying up the kitchen, putting the kettle on for coffee.

The kids were up, and Soo Jin was getting them interested in drawing with crayons on sheets of computer paper. I was glad to see that Mi-Cha and Tae-Yong weren't hitting each other. Neither one of them had mentioned what happened yesterday.

Yun sat at the kitchen table, a pack of Parliaments in front of her. Her brow creased every time she looked at my bruises and scrapes.

I punched numbers into my phone and listened.

Jules picked up, and his pissed-off voice asked, "Hello?"

"It's me, Wes."

"Oh. You all right?"

"Yeah," I said. "Not too bad, considering."

"If you're going to ask me to intervene with these guys again, please don't. They're a bunch of serious assholes. They're starting to annoy me."

"No, don't worry about that. I think we're way past the negotiation stage. If I had a white flag I'd be waving it about right now."

"You're starting to make sense."

"This is what I wanted to ask you. Remember you said I could walk away from the deal, that you'd return my down payment?"

"Offer still stands."

"What about this. You return my down payment, but you let me keep Warsaw Wash."

There was a moment of silence on the phone. Then Jules said, "That doesn't make sense."

I dug in with my pitch. "I'd make accelerated payments on the mortgage. You'd get all your money. I could walk away from this marriage and then just work my balls off paying you back."

There was a pause on the phone, then Jules said, "Wes. I like you. I've grown to consider you almost like a son over the years. But you're missing the big picture. I sold my business for a reason. I needed a cash infusion. I also needed to be with my wife more. She's not doing well at all. When I told you I'd return your down payment that was on the condition that I turn around and sell Warsaw Wash to someone else."

"Yeah, yeah, no, no," I said, backpedaling, feeling like an idiot. "I hear you. I was thinking you might have some room to negotiate."

"I'm not in the position to give nothing away," replied Jules. "You got to face facts here. These Koreans are not like you and me. Asians, they got long, long memories. You know what the Chinese premier said about the French Revolution of 1789? It was the early seventies and he was talking to Nixon. They asked the premier what he thought of the Revolution, and he said, 'It's too early to tell.' Two hundred years later and it was too early to tell. You're dealing with two-ton motherfuckers here. I'm gonna repeat the advice I gave you before. Return the money and run, don't walk, away."

"Jules, I got to tell you, I'm on the fence. I'm not sure which way to jump."

"You better make up your mind soon," said Jules, sounding impatient. "These fuckers are serious sons of bitches. Listen, I gotta go."

I stuck my phone back in my pocket and put the flame under the pot to boil more water.

Yun blew smoke over her shoulder and asked, "How do you feel? You lost a lot of blood yesterday."

That struck me funny. I laughed and said, "Not enough."

TWENTY-NINE

uckily I didn't have to wait too long at the clinic for my hemochromatosis treatment. I hadn't gotten through the one article in *Redbook* that looked interesting—"How to Catch a Cheater"—before they called me back to Room 6.

Royal came into the room and did a double take when he saw my bruised jaw and bandaged brow. "What in hell happened to you?"

"I got jumped."

"A nice boy like you? Who would do that to you?"

"Not everyone shares your opinion."

"Did the police catch them?"

My silence was answer enough. Royal glanced at his wristwatch. "I've got a few extra minutes. Let's take a look under that bandage."

Royal got the bandage off and began cleaning the wound. "That's not too bad," he said. "That's gonna heal good. You in pain?"

"No, not anymore."

"You cut anywhere else?"

"No, but they did a job on my kidneys."

"Are you peeing blood?"

"No."

"Lift your shirt. Let me take a look at your back."

Royal let out a low whistle when he saw the bruises. His fingers probed and prodded. The way he touched me made me uncomfortable. It was more a caress than an examination.

"You're gonna have to keep an eye on that," said Royal. "You start peeing blood or feeling more pain, you get your ass down to the emergency room."

"Got it."

"Did you see the guys who did this to you?"

"A couple of Koreans."

"I wouldn't have thought that," said Royal. "My first guess would have been Mexicans or brothers. Or some of the white trash we have around here. But not Koreans. They don't usually cause this kind of trouble."

"Let's just say that Koreatown is still waters running deep."

Royal arched an eyebrow. "Good-looking and a poet, too. My, my."

I couldn't help laughing at Royal's silly flirting.

"Don't get mad at me, Wes. But did you give them a reason?"

"In their minds, maybe. Not in mine."

"I've been working this clinic for five years. I know a lot of people. Why don't you tell me what's going down. Maybe I can help figure things out."

I thought about it for a second or two. Why should I tell Royal my problems? For all I knew he would treat it as some kind of soap opera. Then I thought—fuck it—I need a second opinion.

Royal hung on every word as I told him the whole story—the blood feud, my marriage to Soo Jin, the murders, how unshakeable Shin was. At the mention of Shin, Royal's eyes widened in surprise.

"That's the man behind this? Shin Doko?"

"You know who he is?"

"He comes to this clinic," replied Royal. "He's not one of my patients. But I heard a lot about him from the other nurses. He causes a lot of heartburn every time he comes in."

"Jesus—he comes in here often? I don't want him seeing me."

"I saw him earlier this week. You got nothing to worry about. Comes in for leukemia treatments."

"Leukemia's like a death sentence, right?"

"Leukemia is a bitch," said Royal. "Your bone marrow starts making all these white blood cells. Mr. Doko is in almost constant pain. We have to keep pumping him full of blood to keep up the count on his red blood cells. He's gonna be dead in five years, Lord have mercy."

I felt a sudden dizziness, thinking of sitting in the same building as Shin, with them drawing blood out of me and pumping blood into him. This was how the world was supposed to work—people helping each other—not the murdering and mayhem.

I shook my head to clear it. "Weird. Shin and I are caught up in a blood feud, and we're both going to the same clinic for our fucked-up blood."

"The Lord is a mysterious player," said Royal.

THIRTY

When I was finished with Royal I drove the few blocks to Warsaw Wash. I took a slow drive by, gratified that cars were lined up for a scrub. I didn't dare go in and instead drove on toward Olympic. I knew I should head back to Yun's and keep a low profile, but I was enjoying the feeling of freedom. As I drove, my mind kept circling the knowledge that Shin and I shared the same clinic. How could I make this work for me? Did it create common ground between both of us? Was it a situation I could manipulate to my own advantage? I thought of Shin sitting in one of those examination rooms with his shirt off, a vulnerable old man. He was the key to all my grief; if I could only turn him.

I hung a left on Olympic and cruised past K-Town's mix of barbecue joints and shopping malls. It was getting close to noon, and the sidewalks were filling with workers heading to lunch. Just when I'd decided I'd pushed my luck enough—that it was time to make tracks for Yun's house—I saw Kwan walking along the sidewalk. I pulled up next to him and lowered the window. "Kwan!"

He turned, surprised to hear his name called out. He recognized me behind the wheel and hurried over to the car.

"Wes, what the fuck are you doing here? We been hearing all kinds of stories." He leaned around to get a better look at my face. "Sounds like they're true, too."

"You got time for lunch?"

"I don't want trouble."

"How much time do you have?"

Kwan couldn't help grinning. "I'm my own boss, you know that."

"Then get in. I'm buying."

Kwan hesitated, looked over his shoulder.

I caught his eye. "Aren't you getting a little tired of Korean food?"

* * *

Kwan scanned El Ranchito's one-page menu. On the table in front of us was a plate of radishes, an assortment of hot-sauce bottles, and a bowl of salsa roja redolent with cilantro and chopped onion. We'd driven over to the heart of East LA, where I felt we were reasonably safe from any search-and-destroy Koreans.

A black-haired waitress, curvy and thick around the middle, came over for our order.

Kwan said, "I'll have the carne asada tacos and a Dos Equis."

I said to the waitress, "Albondigas—that's like a meatball soup, right?"

She nodded and I told her to bring me a bowl, along with a Coke.

When she was gone, Kwan leaned in close and said, "Wes. There's lots of talk about you at Saja. I think there's one asshole who's even taking bets on how long you'll survive. The place isn't the same after Dae-Hyun got his head blown off."

"I wonder about that guy sometimes. I wonder if he knew what kind of danger he was in."

Kwan stabbed at a radish, clumsy with a fork instead of chopsticks. "Word got out that I was your best man."

"That sucks. Are you going to be in trouble over that?"

"I didn't think it was any big deal. But guess who came into the club last night?"

"Who?"

"Shin Doko," said Kwan. "The motherfucker sat down right next to me. It was just when Min Jee was bringing me a bowl of kimchi *jjigae*. I couldn't even eat. Shin asked for the microphone. He sang 'Pyun Ji.'"

"What's 'Pyun Ji'?"

"It's a song about family honor and death. Shin looked at me when he was singing, like he was telling me I was going to die. Fucking song went on forever."

The waitress brought our food and drinks. Kwan ate half a taco in one bite.

"I wish life was simple again," said Kwan. "Eating, drinking, singing. It's nice when a girl sings a love song and looks at you. When Shin sang to me, I could feel his bony fingers around my throat."

"Did he ask you about me?"

"No. As far as I know he didn't even talk to Ms. Tam. Shin was just marking his territory. He had one little glass of soju and left."

"I've tried to negotiate with Shin," I said. "No dice."

"You should move out of LA," said Kwan. "Go somewhere the Koreans haven't settled. Go to Miami, someplace like that."

I tried the albondigas soup. Excellent. Instead of enjoying my lunch I should be worried as hell about Shin. Instead I felt a sense of peace.

I broke up a meatball with my spoon and said, "I miss the Saja Room."

Kwan looked at me like I was crazy. "Don't even think about going there. I'm serious. You should get out of town."

I mulled it over in my mind. Up until today, it was stubbornness that was keeping me from running. Now there was something else mixed up in it. I didn't feel like running away. I liked the people I was with. I liked all of them: Yun, Soo Jin, Mi-Cha, and Tae-Yong. Maybe I even loved them.

"Up until today I've been playing a defensive game," I said, stirring my soup with my spoon. "I think it's time to go on the offense."

Kwan covered his ears with both hands and moaned. "Tell me I'm not hearing this."

* * *

I knew I was pushing my luck, but after dropping Kwan off I drove back to the clinic. I wasn't sure when Royal was finished with his shift but figured there was a good chance he was still working. I parked in the clinic's small lot and watched the door for a minute or two—just because I was being reckless didn't mean I had to be foolhardy. I didn't see anyone coming in or out that I should be worried about. I screwed up my nerve and went inside, straight to the receptionist.

I leaned in close and said, in a conspiratorial whisper, "Hello, ma'am. Earlier today I was in here for my checkup."

"I remember you," said the receptionist.

I guess that wasn't that hard to do, since the number of whites coming through the door were few and far between.

"You see," I said, waving a small piece of paper in my hand. "My nurse, Royal, gave me instructions about a new therapy for my condition. I'd made some notes, but I'm pretty sure that writing them down, I missed something. Could you do me a big favor and just buzz him out here for a second?"

The receptionist stood up. "I'll get him for you."

I watched her disappear along the corridor to the examination rooms. I looked over my shoulder and was gratified to not see anyone that set off alarm bells. This time of the afternoon it was mainly moms with kids.

The receptionist came out trailing Royal. I put my hand on his arm and led him over to a corner.

I said in hushed tones, "The receptionist is here because she thinks I need some medical info. I'm going to hand you a piece of paper with my phone number on it. Call me tonight. It's important."

Royal grinned like a kid receiving a candy bar. "Is this what I think it is?"

"Call me tonight. We have lots to talk about."

"I'm sure we do," said Royal.

THIRTY-ONE

I was sitting in the living room. Yun and Soo Jin were watching a Korean costume drama called *The Moon that Embraces the Sun*, and I was reading Keith Richards's autobiography, *Life*. I was amazed at how smart the man was on the page, since when he spoke he could hardly get out a complete sentence. Keith either had a good ghostwriter or he'd rewired his brain with copious drugs and alcohol in such a way that he was an excellent writer and a mush-mouthed man.

One passage bounced back and forth in my mind, how Keith figured hell and heaven are the same place. What made a hell out of heaven would be sitting up there on a fluffy cloud, but you'd be invisible to your family members—they'd pass you by, not even seeing you. But you could see them. That would be hell.

My cell rang and I picked it up off the table, where it sat next to a cup of green tea and random crumbs from an Oreo cookie.

I heard Royal's voice ask, "Is that you?"

I stood up and walked toward the kitchen. "Hey, man, thanks for calling. Ever since we talked in the clinic I've been thinking."

"I've been wondering myself," said Royal. "You're acting very mysterious. But I have to say, I'm enjoying the way everything is unfolding."

"Do you think we can get together tonight? I'd like to run some ideas by you. One idea mainly."

"I think I could do that for a guy like you."

The flirty tone Royal was taking was making me uncomfortable, but I guess it went with the territory. I asked him where he lived.

"I'm in West Hollywood," answered Royal.

"Is there a good bar near your place? Somewhere we can talk?"

"Scads. How about The Dime? On Fairfax south of Rosewood."

"Great. Thirty minutes?"

"I'll be there."

I hung up and saw Yun staring at me with an intensity she hadn't shown the drama on TV.

"Thirty minutes?" said Yun. "You're going somewhere?"

"I'm going out."

"I heard you," said Yun, frowning. "You're getting together with someone? Who is she?"

"You got it all wrong. It's not like that."

"You can have a hundred women," said Yun. "If that's what you want, go for it. But if you're with me, you're with me only."

Soo Jin looked over her shoulder, as though her fears about Yun and I being together were confirmed. The problem was, Soo Jin lived in a fairy-tale world—it would have been obvious to anyone else by now that Yun and I were fucking each other.

Yun asked, "Who are you seeing?"

"It's not what you think," I said. "It's a guy."

"That's bull," countered Yun. "You were talking to him like you talk to a woman."

"He's a gay guy, all right?" I said, feeling embarrassed. "I learned some important information today. This guy might help me solve our problems."

"Then take me with you," said Yun.

"No. I have to do this by myself."

"You are such a bullshitter."

I waved her into the kitchen, away from Soo Jin. Yun followed me over to the stove, eyes glaring. Part of me liked seeing her jealous. I placed my hands on her shoulders as gently as possible—the last thing I needed was for her to think I was roughing her up.

"Listen," I said. "I'm not playing games. I'm scared for me, I'm scared for you, the kids, Soo Jin. I just want to make things better. I'm going to go see this guy and run a plan by him. Maybe it won't amount to anything. But I've got a target on my back. I don't want to die. I have lots of reasons to live."

"You're not going to die," said Yun. "Not if I can help it."

"Right now, the way I see it, I have two choices—to run or stay. If I stay and hide like a rabbit, I'm going to be chopped. I've been lucky so far, but sooner or later I'm going to fuck up. So please, let me do what I have to do. And don't kick me out of your bed. I need those hours in the middle of the night with you. It's gas in my tank."

"Why can't I go?" said Yun, looking weak. I'd never seen her look anything but strong.

"Don't push my luck," I said as I headed toward the door.

* * *

I parked and walked toward The Dime. Back in the day it was probably just a shot and a beer joint; now LA was lifting nondescript dumps like this into dive-bar status, as though they held some magic of yesteryear. If LA hipsters ever made it out to Pittsburgh, dive bars would lose their charm quick—in some parts of town they were six to a block.

Inside, it took a moment or two for my eyes to adjust to the dim lighting. The juke box was playing a tune I recognized from high school, "What's Luv?" by Fat Joe. I remembered old times driving aimlessly as it played on the radio.

I saw Royal holding down a table for two. He had a bottle of Pabst in front of him, which surprised me. I figured him to be the colorful cocktail type of guy.

He gave me a wave, and I weaved past the drinkers two-deep at the bar. I asked a passing waitress if they had Hite. She said they did, and I asked her to bring one over to the table.

Royal was grinning when I sat down. I'd only seen him in his nurse's whites. Tonight he was wearing a black Hollister T-shirt and a leather beret. The way his eyes shone he might have been wearing a little makeup, too.

"Wes, do you know how often I've been out in the last six months?" asked Royal, with a phony frown. "Zero. I've been so depressed I haven't moved out of the house except for work. I am so thankful you called."

"That's a long time to stay home. Why?"

Royal gestured at his chubby torso. "This. Walter left me because I was too fat. Five years we were together. You'd think that would mean something. When he left me I decided I'd get right back up on the horse and went out to Rage. You know the place?"

"It's a gay disco, something like that, right?"

"Yes. Well I walked in, feeling very confident and a little scared, since I hadn't been cruising for such a long time. The first thing I heard was two boys laughing behind their hands at me. One of them said, 'He'd better be a bottom. If he was a top he'd squash his lover.' I felt crushed, no pun intended, and turned around and left. So, for six long months it's been TV and cookies."

"Well, I'm glad you're feeling good about this."

"How are your bruises?"

"They don't hurt so much anymore."

"You know, a massage is good for the healing process."

The waitress set down my Hite with a knock. Royal watched me take a sip and asked, "Korean beer?"

"I developed a taste for it in the karaoke bars."

"You have many sides, Wes. Many secrets."

"I don't know about that. I'm more the open book type. Not too many secrets."

Royal reached out and tapped my wedding band with a forefinger. "I know many married men who are gay."

Everything got crystal clear real fast. "You think this is a date? Royal, I'm not gay."

I felt terrible seeing the instant sadness transform Royal's face. Seeing this sadness—if I was gay—I would have thrown him a mercy fuck, no problem.

"The story of my life," said Royal. "Always chasing the wrong boy."

"I wasn't trying to lead you on."

"Oh well, now you know more about my lonely life than I ever expected to share." He took a deep pull of his beer and looked at the bottle with displeasure. "I need something sweet." He waved to the waitress and said, *Cuba libre, por favor.*

I said, "Sorry, man."

Royal sighed. "Why did you call me?"

"Because if I don't do something about the situation I'm in, sooner or later I'm going to be dead."

"You mean the situation with the crazy old Korean man and his violent family?"

"I need your help."

"I'm not particularly resourceful that way."

"You wouldn't have to do much."

Royal folded his arms and then said, "Tell me."

I told him. How I had a plan to kidnap Shin Doko. I'd do it when he was being treated at the clinic. Royal's part would be minimal but essential. I'd have Manuel create a distraction in the waiting room. When the nurse was called away from Shin, Royal would slip into the room where Shin was being treated. He'd punch him in the arm with a syringe full of sedative. That's all Royal would have to do. I'd wheel Shin out the back on a gurney.

"Are you going to kill the old man?" asked Royal.

"No. I'm going to kidnap him and bring him to the house where I'm staying. He's going to be my bargaining chip. Maybe the Doko family will listen when one of their own family is in danger."

"First. I can't do it," said Royal. "I could lose my job and go to jail."

"No one has to see you give him the shot. If I get caught, it's all on me. I'll take the syringe you used on Doko and put it in my pocket. I get caught I'll tell them I did it."

"It's a stupid plan. Someone is going to see you."

"I'm going to get me a set of nurse's scrubs. I'll blend right in. I already scoped out the back of the clinic. I can wheel him right out to my car. I'll make it easy."

"They're really going to kill you?"

"They killed the last five of Soo Jin's husbands. It took them a while to warm up to the idea of killing me, but they're definitely going to do it. It's just a matter of time."

"I feel I know you well, Wes. I don't see you being a liar."

"No, this is the truth."

"If I do this for you, I'd be putting myself at considerable risk."

"I'll make it up to you."

"One night of love."

"What?"

"One night of love. I want one night with you, from sundown to sunrise. You'll be my lover, the way I imagined it was going to be when I agreed to meet you tonight."

I realized how desperate I'd become, because for one long moment I tried to imagine myself going through with it.

I remembered an episode of *Fear Factor*, a show where contestants had to face their fears or do disgusting things. I remember one pretty blonde had to eat a raw pig's rectum. It was a tube of corrugated flesh resembling an attachment for a vacuum cleaner.

The hollow tube of flesh made me think of anal sex and how our rectums were hardly the seat of our soul. Seeing that blonde nibbling the pig's rectum, I knew I'd prevail if I ever went to prison and I was gang raped. I'd remember that the tube of corrugated flesh wasn't me—that they weren't raping my soul.

But I wasn't in prison, and I wasn't being raped, and I wasn't going to experience a night of love with Royal.

"Sorry, man," I said. "I can't do that. If I was gay I'd definitely date you, but I'm not gay."

"OK," said Royal. "Then let's explore plan B."

THIRTY-TWO

Yun stared hard at the top of my head and then smacked a hairbrush against the palm of her hand. "It's not easy, trying to make you look gay."

I was sitting on a kitchen chair in the middle of the living room as I tried to transform from working stiff straight guy to glammed-up gay boy. The kids and Soo Jin were having a good old time watching my transformation. I'd shaved super close and rubbed some ChapStick on my lips, making them glossy. A brand-new white T-shirt and my tightest jeans didn't look fey enough—I'd have to add some swish.

Yun swiped at my hair with the brush, trying to give me a tiny pompadour.

"I like you like that," said Soo Jin, trying not to giggle. "You're hot."

Yun smiled. "Yeah, maybe you could show us how you're going to dance."

I grimaced. "Wow…I didn't even think of that. I have a hard enough time dancing with a woman, let alone a guy."

"Now you're going to know how it feels when a guy dances with you and sticks that thing against your leg," said Yun. "I wish I was gonna be there. You're going to learn the hard way."

* * *

Last night, back at The Dime, over a second round of Hites and *cuba libres*, Royal had presented me with his plan B.

142

"I'm nothing if not flexible," said Royal. "If a night of love is not meant to be, then let me propose this. You accompany me to Rage—"

"The gay disco?"

"Yes," said Royal. "I'm so pleased you know Rage."

"I've never been there," I said, probably looking embarrassed. "I must have read about it in the *LA Weekly*."

"Be that as it may, I want you to spend the evening with me as my boyfriend. I've been out of circulation too long. If I show up with a handsome young man who is crazy for me, my stock will shoot through the roof."

"Define *crazy* for me."

"We don't have to kiss. I won't touch your cock. I will grab your ass, and you'll have to look like you're mad for me. If you think people are listening, tell me what a great lover I am. That you're going to miss me when you take that job in New York."

"If I do this, you'll help me with Shin Doko?"

"Yes. But you have to promise to keep me out of it if it all goes to shit."

"It's a deal," I said. "I'll be your boy."

* * *

I stared into the bathroom mirror. Yun had done a good job. If I saw any of my crew at the car wash they would either die laughing or be scared that the sky was falling. Yun had been faced with a somewhat blank canvas to begin with and had transformed me into an acceptably cute guy. I looked five years younger and a lot sexier—if sexy meant Goth eye makeup and a wraparound bandage on my cock, making me look like I was packing a twelve-inch length of PVC pipe.

Yun peeked in and gave me a low wolf whistle. "Don't stay out too late, lover boy. I want to fuck you looking like this."

"I have no idea what I'm walking into," I said. "I may need a hot and sweaty dog fuck when I get home."

"You're gonna have fun and you know it," said Yun, laughing.

Thing is, she was right. For one night I was going to have an inside look at how the other half lives.

* * *

I was lucky—I'd arrived early enough to Rage to claim a space in the parking lot instead of the street. I called Royal on his cell—it occurred to me I didn't know what kind of car he drove.

He answered with, "This is Royal."

"Royal. It's Wes. Are you in the lot?"

"I saw you drive in," answered Royal. "I'm in the red Mini Cooper."

The headlights flashed on a Mini Cooper parked at the far end of the lot.

I said, "I see you."

"Are you ready to escort me in?" asked Royal.

This struck me as being absurd, since Royal had a good three inches on me and about a hundred pounds.

"Sure."

"Act like you're mad about me."

I locked up and walked over to his car. He got out and stood tall, dwarfing his vehicle. He was dressed in a black guayabera with two vertical white stripes, probably in an attempt to slenderize his silhouette.

He gave me the once-over and said, "I love a man with enthusiasm."

* * *

The music was loud and the lights were flashing. I recognized the song as being one by Nicki Minaj where she twerked and sang about an anaconda. It was strange, getting a twinge in my pants thinking about Nicki Minaj while being surrounded by a hundred guys motorboating their behinds around the dance floor. Royal was light on his feet and favored a lot of jazz hand as he danced. I dug deep for my inner gay and imitated some of the simpler moves I saw around me. After a while I began to feel the music and just gave myself over to the bass-heavy beat.

The song ended, and Royal gave me a sweaty hug. He smelled like baby powder. He laughed and said, "Oh, that song is life-affirming in a *bad* way."

I glanced toward the bar, and Royal said, "I agree. Let's get a drink."

As we walked toward the bar, Royal whispered, "Put your hand on my ass."

A deal was a deal, and as we made our way through the crowd I lightly palmed Royal's ass—definitely the biggest one I'd ever grabbed.

Two women smiled at us. When we had entered Rage I'd been surprised to see so many lipstick lesbians. The mix of male to female was the same as any nightclub—the only difference was that it was guy-on-guy and girl-on-girl.

We had to push to get to the bar's edge—it helped that Royal had twice the body mass of those around him.

Royal gestured to the bartender. "Two double *cuba libres*, extra lime."

I noticed Royal's eyes scanning the young men in our immediate vicinity. We both saw two good-looking Asian guys checking us out and pointing, probably trying to sort out the odd matchup Royal and I made.

I leaned in close to Royal. "How am I doing?"

Royal lowered his chin and gave me a playful look. "You know, they say there's no such thing as queer or straight. Everyone's bi. Sexuality is on an adjusting scale."

I thought about that for a second. "I don't know. Maybe. But I think the needle on my scale is way over on the straight side."

"You never know," said Royal.

The DJ shifted into J-Lo's "On the Floor." I remembered how J-Lo looked in that video. I cupped my hand to my mouth and said to Royal, "It's a big world; lots could happen, but I'm still trying to figure out women. I figure it's gonna take me a while."

Our drinks came and Royal made a show of paying.

"Follow me," said Royal. "Let's go to the patio where we can relax."

It was a different feeling being outside. The air was balmy. I could still faintly hear the music from inside. Unlike Koreatown, no one was smoking.

We got lucky—as we walked outside two guys bailed on a table. We sat down and Royal pushed his chair close to mine. He laid a hand on my knee, and for a moment I thought about how embarrassing it would be if someone I knew saw me. Then it occurred to me if they were at Rage, then they were probably gay themselves. Plus, who really cares who's gay and who isn't?

Royal said, "You're enjoying this, aren't you?"

I thought about it for a moment. "Pretty girls. Handsome guys. Good music. Strong drinks." I gestured toward Royal and said, "The company of a friend. What's not to like?"

Royal looked around and then said to me, "I'm coming back tomorrow. I think I've made an impression."

I wondered what Yun was doing right now. Maybe she and Soo Jin were watching TV together. The kids would be asleep. I didn't think I'd be enjoying myself so much without the knowledge that the night would end with me lying next to Yun.

I took a sip of my *cuba libre*—a sweeter drink than I was used to, but not so bad. I looked over my shoulder and saw a Hispanic guy with a little extra fat around his middle giving us the eye. He was at a table of guys who all seemed to be talking at once. I noticed he and Royal did a little flirting with their eyes.

I said, "You're a fun person, Royal. There's no reason you can't find a steady guy."

Royal beamed a smile at me. "Thank you for that, Wes. You know, when Walter left I fell into such a funk. When I'm happy I lose weight. I never get down to being buff, but I'm pleasantly padded if you know what I mean. Being alone I just plump up. No matter how many cookies, it's never enough."

I didn't know what to say so I said nothing.

"I'm still a vital man," said Royal. "I eat all those cookies at night and lay down to bed, and I get a sugar rush hard-on. I lay there in the dark, working away with my eyes closed, and I swear I hear Walter laughing at me. I open my eyes, and I can almost see him in the room—but it's only a shadow. Then it fades away and disappears."

"That's got to ruin the mood."

"What about you?" asked Royal. "Do you ever get lonely?"

"The way I grew up, I think being lonely was the status quo."

"Managed pain," said Royal.

"What do you mean?"

"You learned to live with pain, with being lonely. If you hadn't found a way to manage your pain, you would have gone crazy. It's not a good way to live."

"Maybe not. But that's changing."

"You have your wife," said Royal.

"More than that," I said. "I have my wife and kids and my inamorata."

Royal opened his eyes wide in a comic move. "Wes. You are a constant surprise."

I rattled the ice cubes in my glass. "We've got our own little army."

THIRTY-THREE

It was close to two when I slid into bed next to Yun. She woke up with a start, smiling. She stared at my face, illuminated by the dim light from the street.

"You left it on," she said. "You look so sexy in eye makeup."

"I figure one night won't hurt."

"You smell funny," said Yun. "Like when I'm changing a diaper. Like baby powder."

"Hazards of the night, baby."

"You know you had fun."

"Take charge," I said. "Fuck me like you bought me for the night."

Yun grabbed my cock and got on top, riding me—using me like I was there solely for her pleasure. When I felt she was about to come, I slapped her ass and thrust deeply, taking over and pushing her over the edge.

Yun fell on top of me, exhausted. When she regained her breath, she asked, "What was it like?"

I told her about my night with Royal, making her laugh now and then.

"I think it all went perfect," I said. "I kept my end of the bargain; now it's time for him to deliver."

"Deliver what?" asked Yun.

"I have a plan to turn the tables, but I'm going to keep it to myself. If my plan goes into the toilet, it's better if you and Soo Jin know nothing about it."

"I get worried when you talk like that."

"I don't blame you. But I can't sit here like a target. Sooner or later one of us is going to get hurt. Maybe even one of the kids."

"Don't even say that."

"I'm going to do everything I can to keep anything like that from happening."

"Mi-Cha was asking about you tonight, where you were."

I thought about that and it made me feel good. "She's a sweet little girl."

"You don't have to do much to get their love," said Yun. "They're going to adopt you."

"That was quick."

"Little kids need a father," said Yun. "Mi-Cha and Tae-Yong don't even have a grandfather. You have to be careful—don't play with their hearts."

I thought about my own father. "Don't be afraid to give me a few tips on how to be a parent."

Yun pointed at the bedside table. "Hand me your wallet."

I reached over and gave it to her. She reached in and took out a dollar bill.

Yun scooted her ass to the middle of the bed and said, "Now fuck me like you paid for it."

* * *

The next morning I waited until it was quiet. Yun was off to work, the kids were playing in the backyard, and Soo Jin was in the bathroom washing her hair. I called Manuel and told him things were heating up, that I didn't feel safe leaving the house in the daytime. He needed to come over to Yun's so I could run something by him.

He showed up at the door a couple of hours later, with a bag of carne asada tacos and a quart of Tecate. He held up the bag. "Early lunch, homes. Enough for two." He heard Soo Jin in her room and said, "Should I have brought more?"

"No worries, man. I'll split mine with Soo Jin. She'll probably like it. Carne asada's kind of like Korean barbecue anyway."

I got a couple of plates and glasses, and we laid out lunch. I put aside a taco for Soo Jin.

Manuel reached for the bottle of hot sauce. "In case you're wondering, everything is *suavecito* at Warsaw Wash."

"I got complete faith in you," I said. "Thanks for keeping things humming."

"Jules had you," replied Manuel. "I figure sooner or later you're going to need a right-hand man. Make it official."

"There's a couple more laps to go, but you've got the inside track," I said. "No one else is even close."

The carne asada taco was more than I expected, with guacamole, chopped onions, and jalapeños. I took a bite. "The Koreans have had me on the run. Problem is, sooner or later they're going to catch me. I can't stay holed up here forever."

"I see where you're going with this," said Manuel.

"I guess you would."

"You see it in the barrio," said Manuel. "You don't protect what's yours, they take it away. Sometimes you got to cowboy up."

I glanced toward Soo Jin's room—the door was still closed. I lowered my voice. "I've told you about the clinic I go to every week, because of the iron in my blood. I found something out a few days ago. The top dog trying to kill me goes to the same clinic. His name is Shin Doko. I'm going to kidnap the motherfucker."

"That's heavy time, homes."

"If I fuck it up, yes. But these Koreans don't go to the police. They handle things on their own. Shin Doko's going to be my bargaining chip."

"How you gonna do it?"

"I've got someone on the inside, inside the clinic."

Manuel looked down with sad eyes at his empty plate. Maybe he was sad his lunch was finished, but I was almost certain he was sad because he knew what I was going to ask next.

"I'm not going to be able to do it by myself," I said. "I'm going to need help."

Manuel looked up and said, "I'm your man."

* * *

Royal called me later that day and told me that Shin would be in tomorrow for an afternoon appointment. Manuel and I would have to wait in place from two on and be ready to move fast when we got Royal's call. I told him we'd be there.

The rest of the day and night passed in a blur. Yun snapped at me once or twice for not answering simple questions. The kids gave me funny looks, like I'd turned into somebody else—someone they didn't know. Soo Jin was unchanged in her reaction to me, which made me realize that my current mental state was probably one she lived in 24/7—here but not here.

As night fell I finally gave up and settled into the couch. A passenger of Yun's had left an Adam Sandler DVD in the back of her taxi. I put it on and watched it over and over. Even after three viewings I still couldn't tell you what I saw.

Just like Soo Jin, I was here but not here.

THIRTY-FOUR

I sat in my Jeep Cherokee in the parking lot behind the clinic, dressed in a plastic rain poncho. I had my cell phone on the dash, fully charged. On the seat next to me was a plastic bag from the 99 Cents store filled with stuff I thought I might need: duct tape, a length of rope, a black hood, and a knife. My sawed-off shotgun was under the seat. I felt like I was in a scene in a straight-to-DVD movie, one of those with an actor on a downward trajectory, like Val Kilmer or Christian Slater. I was definitely in one-step-at-a-time territory. First I had to get Shin in the car. Once I got him home, I had to figure out how to get the most out of my bargaining chip. Maybe I could convince Mi-Cha and Tae-Yong that Shin was their grandfather; I'd have a hard time explaining why I was keeping grandpa tied up.

Before I'd driven in I'd spray-painted the lens of the parking lot's security camera. Royal had told me it was mostly there for show and was rarely in operation, but I wasn't taking any chances.

I looked at my phone: it was twenty after two. Manuel had confirmed he was in the waiting room, holding the Big Gulp from the 7-Eleven. Royal had refused to talk to me on my cell since we made the plan—he was smart enough to know that if this thing went south the police would be checking my phone records. The signal was for him to walk out to his car and pick up a book he'd promised to lend to another nurse. That's when I'd know to come in the back door of the clinic, which was only occasionally locked.

Yun had taken the day off and was at home with Soo Jin and the kids. She knew I was executing a serious maneuver and had given up trying to get the details out of me. She'd said, "I'm gonna be here waiting if you decide you need me." Then she'd gone back to making lunch for the kids. I had a feeling that no matter what I did with my life I'd be stronger with Yun at my side.

Royal came through the door, giving me only the barest of glances. He walked stiff-legged, as though his limbs were coursing with adrenaline. He walked over to his car, beeped it open, and took a book out of the back seat. I watched him walk back in and disappear behind the door.

I called Manuel. He picked up, and I said, "It's on you, bro."

I slipped the poncho over my head. I was dressed in burgundy hospital scrubs, the same as the other nurses at the clinic. I glanced at the back seat, where I had a pillow propped up against the side-door window. No sense breaking Shin's neck on the ride home.

I walked in the back way, glancing into the break room, where I saw Royal in serious conversation with a female nurse, a black woman. I'm not sure what Royal was telling her, but I could see he had her complete attention. I kept walking down the short hall, looking in one room after another. At the end of the hall I could see into the waiting room, where a commotion was in full swing. I caught a glimpse of Manuel, waving his arms in a frenzy—a spray of blood covering his chest. I was the only person who knew it wasn't blood—it was catsup mixed with chunks of pork fat. His Big Gulp was filled with it. On my phone signal he had filled his mouth with the mess and sprayed it down his chest, imitating a full-blown hemorrhage. He was topping off the bloody display with a top-of-the-lungs reggaeton rap about being the biggest gangsta in East LA. I knew I had only a minute or two before Manuel bolted out the front door. We were depending on no one chasing him. This is LA after all. They'd be glad he was off and running and on his way to being someone else's problem.

Looking in an examination room, I saw Shin's bony face pointing up at the ceiling. There was a gurney outside the door. I wheeled it in next to the examination table. Shin looked to be out cold from the shot Royal gave him. To make sure, I pinched him on the arm: nothing—no response at all.

I slid him from the table to the gurney. It was easy—I don't think he weighed more than 150 pounds. The commotion reached a crescendo in the waiting room and then silence. Manuel was most likely booking down the sidewalk toward the car he'd parked on the other side of the block.

I didn't have a second to waste. I wheeled Shin toward the back door—not too fast, not too slow. I'd shifted Shin's face so he was turned away from the break room. I blocked it further with an outstretched arm as we rolled past, where Royal was still in deep, deep conversation with the female nurse.

I got the gurney through the back door and to my car, where I hustled Shin's body into the back seat.

I took a quick look around. Cars were driving by, but there was no one walking past taking a curious look at a male nurse doing weird things with what looked to be a dead body.

I got behind the wheel, slipped back into my rain poncho, and told myself to be calm as I fired up the engine.

I pulled into traffic and glided down Western Avenue.

Taking a quick glance back at Shin, I saw his eyes wide open, looking pissed as could be.

THIRTY-FIVE

It's not easy steering a car with your left hand while holding a sawed-off shotgun with your right. Leaning back over the seat and pressing the barrel against the gut of a bony old man. Shin was still under the effect of the anesthesia, otherwise I'm sure he'd have used some arcane martial art to wrest the gun away and blow my head off.

He still hadn't said a word. Instead he glared at me, breathing hard.

I felt silly wearing a cheap plastic rain poncho on a sunny day, but I didn't want anyone to see me in burgundy scrubs.

We only had a few blocks to go to get to Yun's house when Shin said, "You're a dead man."

I gave his belly a light jab with the shotgun. "Don't fuck with a dead man."

That shut him up.

I pulled into Yun's driveway; I'd asked her to keep it clear for me. I saw her black Camry parked out front. I'd weighed having Manuel meet me here, to help me get Shin inside, but then had thought better of it. There was no sense bringing Manuel that far into my problems. I didn't want Manuel to be looking over his shoulder, wondering when he'd get whacked by the Koreans. The way it stood now, 100 percent of the blame was on me. I was going to keep it that way.

Glancing over at the living room window I saw the shade move.

I turned off the engine and pocketed my keys. I felt more capable having my attention focused on only one thing—getting Shin inside.

I locked on to Shin's pale eyes. "You said it yourself, I'm a dead man. I've seen firsthand what happens to guys who marry Soo Jin. I'm jumpy as all hell. So, think hard. Do you want to fuck with a scared guy like me, when he has a shotgun in his hands?"

Shin asked, "What is it you want me to do?"

"For now, I want you to walk into that house in front of me."

"I'm not sure I can walk. The drugs…"

"You can't walk, I'll drag you. One way or another we're going into the house. Quick."

The side door of the house opened, and Yun appeared on the step, shading her eyes, peering at the car. She started walking toward us.

I gestured with the gun at Shin and warned, "No bullshit."

I got out, and Yun gave me the once-over. "You look crazy." Then she saw the gun in my hand and asked, alarmed, "What's going on?"

I opened the back seat door and gripped Shin by his wizened bicep. "Let's go."

He was wobbly, but able to stand. I kept my hand on his arm as I marched him toward the house. Without his bodyguards and Lincoln Continental, Shin was nothing more than a skinny old Korean dude.

Yun's eyes were wide as she asked, "You took him?"

"Then you know who he is?"

"Of course."

"Get the plastic bag from the front seat."

Shin stared at Yun as she grabbed the plastic bag from the 99 Cents store. He said, "Tell this white fool to let me go."

"Hey," I warned. "Leave the racist remarks outside on the street. I don't want the kids hearing that kind of poison."

I remembered my dad, with his half-drunk slurs. Sitting in front of the TV, spouting off about the niggers and the kikes and the wetbacks. I'd swallowed that stuff whole until I was twelve or so. I then began sorting things out on my own. Eventually I came to my own conclusion—that we were all human beings, capable of hitting the high notes or getting down into the mud. It all came down to individual will, and that had nothing to do with what color you were. No matter where you looked, in every race there was plenty of bad and a little good and a lot of in-between.

I nudged Shin aside. "Yun, open the door."

Yun slipped past me and got the door open. I led Shin inside the house. Soo Jin was huddled with the kids on the far side of the dining room table. I still had the shotgun hidden from view under my poncho—I didn't want the kids to see the gun if I could help it.

I gestured toward Soo Jin and said, "Get the kids into their room."

Soo Jin didn't take her eyes off Shin as she led the kids away and closed the door to their room. With the kids out of the way she stared at Shin with an expression that mingled fear and anger. I can't say I blamed her. Shin was the architect behind her persecution—the blame was on his head.

I sat Shin down on the couch and stepped back.

"You are a fool," said Shin.

Trouble was, dressed the way I was, I felt like a fool.

"Yun, do me a favor. Get me my T-shirt and jeans. They're on the chair in the bedroom."

I stripped off the poncho and scrubs and stood in front of Shin in my white briefs, the shotgun in my hand.

Shin looked me up and down. "You have no dignity."

"Yeah?" I said. "Maybe you have too much."

Yun handed me my clothes. I kept one eye on Shin as I dressed, feeling more capable out of my disguise and in my own clothes.

"You should have told me," said Yun.

"Right now, everything is going my way," I said. "If I'd told you, who knows what would have happened."

"But this is my house."

"Don't pull that one on me," I said, a pissed-off tone creeping into my voice. "You took me in. When you did, you took in my problems, too." I pointed at Shin. "My biggest problem is right there."

"Are you going to kill him?" asked Soo Jin.

"You know how to use a shotgun?"

Soo Jin looked at me like I was crazy. "No."

I held the gun up. "Yun?"

Yun took the shotgun from me, checked to see if the safety was off, and then aimed it at the wall above Shin's head.

"I guess so," I said.

I took the duct tape out of the bag and pointed at Shin. "Stand up."

I picked up a plastic Transformers toy from a McDonald's Happy Meal and tossed it at Shin. He caught the toy in his right hand and then dropped it to the floor. So, he was right-handed.

Pointing a finger at him I warned, "I'll knock you out if you try anything stupid."

I wrapped the tape around his body and right arm, pinning it to his side. With a length of rope I made a hobble around his ankles, enough so he could take tiny steps.

Stepping back, I surveyed my work. It would do for now, as long as someone kept an eye on him at all times.

"You mess around with the tape, or try and fuck with me, I'm going to tape you solid," I said. "With one hand free, you can feed yourself, pee, wipe your ass—all that stuff. I love this family too much to ask them to do that."

"What are you going to do to him?" asked Yun.

"Give me the shotgun back."

The question in Yun's eyes was obvious, and I said, "No, I'm not going to shoot him."

I took the shotgun and put it away in the bedroom. I didn't want the kids to see we had a gun in the house.

Yun was standing by the doorway to the kids' room when I came back out. "They can't stay locked up in their room," said Yun. "You leave a question in a kid's mind and they're gonna fill it up with their fears."

I opened the door and said, "Come on out, kids."

Mi-Cha marched out and Tae-Yong toddled after her.

I pointed at Shin. "This man is going to be staying with us for a while. His name is Shin Doko."

"Why is he tied up?" asked Mi-Cha.

"It's a kind of game," answered Yun.

"Is he our grandfather?" asked Mi-Cha.

"No, just a man," said Yun.

I asked Shin, "You want a glass of water?"

He nodded.

I got him a glass from the tap and handed it to his left hand. He drank it down in a series of refined gulps.

"You taking medicine?" I asked.

"In my pocket," answered Shin.

"Take it out."

He handed me a bottle of prednisone, and I placed it on the mantel. I said, "You let me know when you need a dose."

"Let me go now," said Shin. "And I'll give you a day to run away. We can pretend this never happened. You can divorce Soo Jin and run."

I had to hand it to Shin. Here he was, bound hand and foot, and he's talking about giving me a head start. "This is your problem, Shin. You and your family climbed up on your high horse centuries ago. It's time you climbed down and lived in the modern world. As stupid and primitive as your point was, you made it. The Nang family is decimated."

"You act like two and two equals five," responded Shin.

"I don't think so."

"There is only one solution," said Shin. "The blood feud is over when every Nang is dead."

"Maybe you're the solution," I said. "Maybe this is over when you're dead. Maybe the rest of the Doko clan doesn't have the stomach for seeing their own family members killed off one by one."

Shin stuck his chin out at me. "Two and two is four."

"You ever play chess, Shin?" I asked. "It's over when you checkmate the king."

THIRTY-SIX

I thought Yun would be embarrassed when I asked her to run the errand for me. Instead she laughed—the first laugh or smile I'd gotten out of her since I'd shown up with Shin.

I opened my wallet and handed her a fifty. "That ought to cover it."

"I wish you were going with me," she said. "We might get some good ideas."

She drove off, heading toward the Pleasure Chest on Santa Monica, where she would pick up a pair of bondage handcuffs. We were going to have to sleep sometime. I figured I'd handcuff Shin to the pipe under the kitchen sink. He wouldn't be comfortable, but with a pillow and blankets it wouldn't be torture, either.

I'd never played a musical instrument, but the feeling I was having was probably similar to what a jazz musician feels when he leaps into a long solo. He doesn't know where it's going to end—at most it's a burst of notes at a time, one burst following another. I was a musician in the middle of a solo. I had Shin Doko—it was going my way—but I was unsure of my next burst of notes. I figured right about now every last member of the Doko clan was scouring Koreatown for their patriarch.

I'd shifted Shin over to the easy chair in the living room so the family could use the sofa to watch TV. He sat there, the corners of his mouth drooping in a permanent frown. His thinning hair had got messed up, and a few oiled strands stuck up.

My cell buzzed. Manuel.

Manuel said, "I tried calling before, but you didn't pick up."

"I had my hands full." I walked into the kitchen, keeping one eye on Shin. "I saw you through the window to the waiting room. You were very convincing."

"Homes, they were so scared of me. I was like something out of a scary movie. I had the blood all down my front. The pig fat hitting the floor. Man, it looked ugly."

"Let's make it official. You're my number two. My manager. You stepped up big time. I owe you."

"Thanks. I won't let you down. You get the old dude to your house?"

"Yeah."

"What are you gonna do now?"

"You got any ideas?"

"No, you're in outer space now, homes. You're on your own."

I hung up and sat on the couch.

Soo Jin peeked from the doorway of the kids' room and then came out with Mi-Cha and Tae-Yong. They climbed up on the sofa with me as Soo Jin got together a bowl of green grapes from the kitchen. It was quiet in the house, the way a house can be quiet in the late afternoon. Soo Jin handed the bowl of grapes to Mi-Cha and picked up the remote.

Jamjari barked from the backyard, a signal he was lonely and wanted to come in. I opened the back door, and Jamjari licked my hand in gratitude. Shin's eyes went wide when he saw the mastiff.

I pointed at Jamjari and said to Shin, "Don't do anything to piss us off."

I sat back down on the couch. Soo Jin was a genius with the remote. We watched *Dog Whisperer*. Something even Jamjari would like.

* * *

Dinner was strange. I served Shin first. A knife and fork would have been difficult, but it was easy for him to handle chopsticks with one hand. He'd asked for a beer, and Yun had gone out for a six of Hite. She popped the tab for him, something Shin had trouble doing with his left hand.

I sat at the far end of the table as Shin picked at his meal. Neither one of us said anything. Shin ate slowly, with consideration, but the look in his eyes told me it was a cinch his belly would be hurting later on. He was looking at me with such hate that I could imagine his stomach churning with acid as he digested his dinner.

After he was finished eating, Yun put together a makeshift bed on the kitchen floor, and I handcuffed Shin to the pipe under the kitchen sink. I considered releasing him from the loops of duct tape securing his right hand against his body and then thought better of it. With his right hand free, too many things could go wrong.

Later, when I was standing in the living room I had a clear sight line into the kitchen. I was surprised to see Yun bend down and hold a glass of water to Shin's lips. For a second there was almost a feeling of tenderness between them. It was amazing the hold these old Korean dudes had over those younger than them. I wondered if they earned that kind of respect and consideration, or if it was something handed to them with no strings attached, just by virtue of being an elder. With Shin in the house, thoughts of my own father kept popping into my head. I tried to imagine doing something nice for him, like Yun had just done for Shin, and my brain stalled out. I couldn't see myself being sweet with my dad. It made me wonder if some of the fault lay with me. Maybe I could have been a better son.

I grabbed one of the Hites from the fridge and slipped out to the backyard. It was a moonless night, and the extra layer of dark made me feel safe and concealed. I sat down at Yun's battered patio table and pulled up a white plastic chair. The night was quiet enough. I could hear some traffic noise and faint music from a neighboring house, a song I recognized as "Seven Nation Army" by The White Stripes.

I dug my phone out of my pocket and placed it on the table. It sat there for a few minutes until I picked it up and punched some numbers. He answered on the second ring, and I said, "Hi, Dad."

"Wes?"

"Is it too late to call?"

"No, I'm up. But don't make a habit of calling me this late."

When I imagined Shin Doko in his home, I always imagined him wearing a suit and tie, sitting in a severe and ordered living room, watching a business program on cable. With my dad, it was too easy to see him on a stained couch in the dark, lit only by the light from the TV tube, drinking beer and eating pickles from the jar. Him and his pickles. He said they provided alkalinity to the acidity of the beer. By the end of the night, his white T-shirt would be decorated with yellow-green streaks of pickle juice.

Months would usually go by between my calls. My dad must have wondered why I was calling so soon—it had only been a couple of weeks since our fucked-up conversation about my Chevy Nova.

I said, "I thought I'd catch you up with a few things."

"Like what?"

"Remember I told you I wanted to buy that car wash? I was able to pull it together. I have my own business now."

There was a pause on the line. Then, "Really?"

"Yeah, Warsaw Wash. I'm keeping the old name."

"Koreatown, right?"

"Yeah, but this place was around a long time before the neighborhood went Korean."

"Twenty-five and you got your own business? That's fuckin' amazing."

I thought about telling him about my new bride, but then I felt I'd have to tell him about Yun, too. And Mi-Cha and Tae-Yong. The fact that all of them were Korean. I figured I'd leave that ball of wax for another day.

"So you've got employees?"

"Yeah. Six of them. All of them are Mexicans."

"Mexicans are hard workers."

"Yeah. The guys I grew up with? Most of them wouldn't last a day washing cars by hand."

My dad said, "Your generation is soft. They got extra-strong thumbs from playing video games and that's about it. The Chinese ever invade us, it's gonna be the blacks and the Mexicans turning them back."

"I think those days are over, Dad. It's all drones and smart bombs now."

"Technology can only take you so far. You got Chinese running through your yard, you're gonna want a tough son of a bee watchin' your back."

I wondered how many beers my dad had downed. Even so, it was the first conversation we'd shared in a long while. Usually it was an exchange of info, then over and out.

"I think I can take care of my backyard," I said. "I bought myself a sawed-off a few days ago."

"What kind?"

"A Remington 870."

"That's a good gun." I could hear the approval in his voice. "You're growing up, son. Next thing you're gonna tell me you found a broad to settle down with."

"Let's leave something for next time."

"Send me some photos of the car wash. I want to see what you're doing."

After I hung up, I took a deep pull from my can of beer. Maybe I caught him in the aftermath of a Hallmark commercial. Maybe he was changing.

Maybe I was changing.

THIRTY-SEVEN

The next morning found me bleary-eyed. It had been a sleepless night. My mind wouldn't shut down. It kept circling the fact that I was a kidnapper—that I was sitting on a powder keg. But as I set my feet on the floor, I knew that as bleary-eyed as I was, Shin had to be a thousand times worse. A guy his age must be a bundle of aches and pains after spending the night on a linoleum floor. I looked over and saw that Yun was out cold. My tossing and turning had kept her up, too, until the dawn started breaking and she crashed out of sheer weariness.

Slipping on some jeans and a T-shirt, I padded into the kitchen. Shin was wide awake, sitting with his back to the fridge, glaring at me.

"It didn't have to go this far," I said.

"Fuck you, white ghost."

"Ghost? Is that the best you got?"

"Round eye."

"You're getting there."

I looked over and saw Soo Jin staring at both of us. She had a spooky way of appearing next to me without making a sound.

"I'm going to have to cut this guy loose," I said to Soo Jin. "You up for helping me out?"

She nodded.

"You don't have to be scared of him," I said. "He's a sick old man. He's gonna be six feet in the ground when you're taking your kids to Disneyland."

"What do you want me to do?" asked Soo Jin.

"Wait here a minute."

I went into the bedroom and got the shotgun, duct tape, and the keys to the handcuffs.

"We're going to do permanent damage to his circulation if we keep him tied up the same way. I want you to free his right hand and tape up his left the same way—see how I got it wrapped around?"

"Yes," said Soo Jin.

I opened the cutlery drawer and handed her a serrated steak knife.

"Cut through the duct tape."

I pointed the gun at Shin. "You fuck with her and I'll kill you. I'll feed you to the dog. Got that?"

Shin tried another angry glare, but the wattage dimmed and fluttered like lights in a power failure. He stared down at the floor, looking every inch the old man he was.

Soo Jin trembled as she worked the knife through the duct tape.

"He's not going to hurt you," I said.

Shin had sweat under the tape, and a rank odor wafted up. Soo Jin kept cutting. Then I saw her gag—hesitate—then lurch to her feet and hurl a load of sour vomit into the sink, splashing all over last night's dinner dishes.

I stepped to the side so I'd have a clear shot if Shin made a move. "Yun!"

Yun came running out of the bedroom in nothing but red panties. She was a sight.

"It was too much for Soo Jin," I said. "Help her and come back. I need you here."

Yun put an arm around Soo Jin and helped her to the bathroom.

Shin looked down and wrinkled his nose at a splash of vomit on his pants.

I said, "You're quite the ladies' man, Shin."

Yun came back in a robe and said, "She's all right. What do you want me to do?"

I told her the same thing I told Soo Jin, and Yun had it done in a flash, with Shin wrapped up the reverse of yesterday.

Soo Jin reappeared and sat on the sofa, looking wan and wasted.

I gestured with the shotgun toward the easy chair and said to Shin, "Sit your ass down and try not to make anyone puke."

* * *

Ms. Tam must have spent the afternoon at the beauty parlor. Her carefully coiffed black hair was shorter and looked to be her own instead of a wig. Her lipstick was red, and her nails shone with clear lacquer. The sheath dress she wore was a blue metallic fabric that accentuated her curves. All in all, she was looking good, period—no matter what her real age was.

I hadn't asked her for a meeting, and when I showed up at her door unexpectedly she hustled me inside, looking pissed and scared at seeing me.

"Why do you come here?" she said, eyes flashing. "Especially now, after what you've done."

I followed her into her chrome and glass living room and said, "I have to talk to somebody."

"Everyone is gossiping about the kidnapping," complained Ms. Tam. "It's made people so upset that some are speaking about going to the police."

"What was I supposed to do?" I countered. "Roll over and let them blow my head off? Run away and give up my business? And what about Soo Jin? Why does she have to live with this hanging over her head the rest of her life?"

I thought these sensible questions would dial down Ms. Tam's anger. Instead she got even more heated. "You are a fool," she said. "And I was a fool to bring an outsider into this."

"Maybe," I said. "But I knew what I was doing marrying Soo Jin. It wasn't your fault."

"There are rules," she said. "You're like someone doing a crazy dance in the middle of a ballet."

Hearing this, I felt like I'd parachuted into an alternate reality. "Ballet? You call someone getting their head blown off a ballet? With all due respect, Ms. Tam, stop the bullshit. You got paid. I got paid. We had a problem from day one. Now we got an even bigger problem."

"You made it worse."

"All right. I made it worse. You made your point. What do we do now?"

"First, never come here again."

I listened, but I wasn't making any promises.

Ms. Tam asked, "Is Shin Doko still alive?"

"I'm not going to kill Shin," I said. "I'm not a killer."

"He's an old man. The shock might kill him."

"Maybe. But he's doing all right."

"His family wants him returned, unharmed."

"I figured that. What do I get out of the deal?"

"You will be allowed to leave Los Angeles."

I let out a deep breath, tired of the stubborn Doko family. They had so much pride and so much power. I'd let the air out of their tires, and they were oblivious, riding along on the rims.

I leaned in closer to Ms. Tam and said, "If I cut off one of Shin's ears and send it to the Dokos in a jar of kimchi, you think that'll get their attention?"

Spittle flew out of her mouth when she answered, "Don't be an asshole."

"I'm not running," I said. "I've got lots of reasons to stay."

Ms. Tam looked at her watch and said, "It's three o'clock."

She walked into the kitchen and came back with a green bottle of soju and two glasses. She poured and handed one to me.

"You were a polite young man," she said. "This has changed you."

"I had everything under control, Ms. Tam. I did everything in moderation. I kept things so moderate you'd probably have had a hard time finding a pulse. Things have changed. I'm not alone anymore."

"You fell in love with Soo Jin?"

"Not exactly. I feel responsible for her." I was about to tell her about Yun but stopped myself.

"I don't know if you can appease the Doko family, no matter what you do," said Ms. Tam. "They revere Shin. If you harm him they'll never stop until you're dead. So be very careful."

"Will they deal with me?"

"The Dokos are cunning. If they make a deal with you, examine it from every angle. They'll do their best to create a path that will leave them free to persecute you and Soo Jin."

I took a sip of the soju, feeling it burn my throat.

Ms. Tam asked, "Are you still in Koreatown?"

"Yeah, I am."

"Then you're not safe," said Ms. Tam.

"But what am I supposed to do?"

"I've told you what to do. Run."

"I can't do that."

Ms. Tam stood up. My visit was over.

"There will be more than Dokos looking for you now," said Ms. Tam. "They will have hired professionals to hunt you."

THIRTY-EIGHT

The afternoon sun was mellow coming through the bamboo blinds. Shin's eyes followed Tae-Yong as he toddled around the room. Tae-Yong had made up a game with a piece of crumpled paper. He'd throw it on the floor, grin, then pick it up. He was working his way across the room, finding his own joy. I wondered what a stranger would think of this tableaux: a white guy on the sofa, an old Korean dude bound with duct tape, and a little kid throwing a ball of paper around the room. I had a feeling it would be a while before it was duplicated anywhere else in the world.

I picked up my iPad and did a Google search. In less than a minute I had the number and info I was looking for. I dug out my phone and made the call.

A polite voice answered, "Sharper Image."

"I'm looking for a karaoke system," I said. "Do you have the GPX Party Machine? Can I get that delivered today? Is that possible?"

* * *

The truck rolled up around four-thirty. In a half hour I had the machine set up in the living room. Soo Jin and the kids watched with interest; I think even Shin was intrigued. I turned it on, picked up the mic, and said, "Test…testing."

I laid the mic down and said to Soo Jin, "Let's wait until Yun gets home before we give it a full-blown test-drive."

I'd called Yun near the end of her cab-driving shift and asked her to pick up some ice cream, some soju, a twelve-pack of beer, Famous Franks, hotdog buns, and a bag of chips.

She'd asked me what the occasion was, and I said, "It's time for a party."

* * *

Yun stood in the middle of the room, belting out a note-perfect rendition of "Yesterday." Her kids stared in rapture. Later she told me it was the first time they'd heard her really sing. Yun was dressed for a party, in blue cowboy boots, brief shorts with the word *Juicy* emblazoned across the backside, and a mint-green T-shirt adorned with a silver appliqué of a setting sun. She looked beautiful and happy as she sang.

Everyone applauded when Yun finished. Yun almost skipped across the room and landed in my lap. Manuel gave me an approving nod—he'd seen our slow-motion romance at Warsaw Wash and was pleased we were together.

Kwan handed his glass of soju to Min Jee and picked up the mic from the stand. It was his turn to sing, and he picked a Korean ballad. As the first bars played, he gave a slight bow and said, "This song is for you, Mr. Doko, and for our homeland. "'Arirang.'"

I could see Kwan was hedging his bets and playing it smart. Nothing wrong with trying to get on Shin's good side.

Yun leaned close to my ear and said, "It's a very old song, almost like our national anthem. About lovers in the Land of Dreams."

I'd thought hard about the wisdom of inviting a few friends over. Was I putting them in danger? I decided to invite them while giving them the caveat that they might see my head blown off during the festivities, and some of the blame for the trouble I was causing might stick to them. I also told them that they had to keep their mouths shut about a few things—that I'd explain once they were here. Whether they showed or not was up to them.

Koreans love a party. Mexicans love a party. The only one who didn't show was Ms. Tam. She'd hung up on me before I got the full invitation out of my mouth. Kwan's jaw had dropped when he saw Shin, but I could tell he was enjoying the high drama of it all.

Kwan had pulled me aside and said, "You've done it now. You're walking on the tiger's tail."

Min Jee had made a beeline for the GPX Party Machine. She'd immediately adjusted the mic so there would be plenty of reverb. The presence of a duct-taped and hobbled Shin Doko didn't seem to faze her. Instead she took it on herself to make sure Shin's hot dog was prepared the way he liked it, and his glass of soju was regularly topped off. She treated Shin like a customer who had rolled into the Saja Room in a wheelchair.

Yun felt warm in my lap—I felt like I was holding nature's bounty. It was a good feeling. Seeing the kids eating potato chips and hearing people laugh. Seeing Soo Jin break into a smile or two. Even with all its problems, the life I was living now beat grinding out nights alone in a small room, reading about other people's lives—people who actually amounted to something.

Kwan finished, and I called out, "Soo Jin. Let's hear something from you."

Yun shifted in my lap so I could stand up. I took the mic from Kwan and held it out toward Soo Jin. "Come on. I have a feeling you love to sing."

Soo Jin was dressed in one of her simple shifts, this one white trimmed with blue. She'd made an attempt at putting on makeup. Her eyes were shadowed with blue, and her lipstick was a brown shade of red.

Soo Jin took the mic and said, "I'll sing, but Wes, you have to sing with me."

Before I could say yes or no Kwan had handed me the second mic.

I asked, "What are we going to sing?"

Soo Jin said, with a nod toward Min Jee sitting next to the machine, "'Sweet Caroline.'"

The opening notes of the Neil Diamond song began to play, and Soo Jin took the first verse, singing about not knowing where it all began.

We both sang the chorus, with our arms around each other's waists.

Manuel and Kwan sang along from their seats.

I looked at Yun, smiling with pleasure.

Life could be easy if the Dokos faded away. Lots of singing, drinking beer on the patio, watching a bootleg DVD, slow nights with Yun in bed, waking up for work.

It was an impromptu party on a weekday, and it ran out of gas a few minutes shy of midnight. People were finishing their drinks as I walked around, picking up plates and crumpled napkins. The kids were asleep on the couch. I walked over to put away the karaoke machine when I heard Shin say, "I haven't sung yet."

It was the first thing Shin had said all evening. Kwan and Min Jee had directed comments at him and hadn't pushed when they'd received no response.

"You want to sing?" I asked.

"Yes."

The others gathered around. Kwan poured himself another soju. I handed the mic to Shin.

"'My Way,'" said Shin.

I punched in the number, and Shin bobbed his head in time to the opening bars of the Sinatra tune. It was weird to see Shin holding the mic with his left hand, his right arm duct-taped to his side. He straightened and then began to sing, about facing the final curtain.

Shin had a good voice, and you could tell it was a song he'd sung many times before. But there was no humility in the way he sang—he sounded like he was addressing the troops.

And I felt fear for the first time that day, when Shin glared at me as he attacked the lyric, the line about eating it up and spitting it out.

THIRTY-NINE

The morning after the party, Yun and I were the first ones up. I got Shin unhooked from the kitchen sink and settled in the living room. Yun and I had tidied up before going to bed, but here and there lay a stray paper plate or balled napkin.

I tied up the trash bag and hauled it out to the cans. Walking back, I could see through the window Yun handing a cup of tea to Shin. They seemed to be having a serious conversation. Maybe she was trying to break through the old man's reserve. If anybody could do it, Yun could. She was a joy to be around, especially in the morning. Yun had the gift of waking up as though each day was a clean slate.

As I rinsed my hands in the kitchen sink, Yun came up behind and gave me a hug.

"That was a good party," said Yun.

"Those were the first guests I've had since I moved to LA," I said. "I wouldn't mind doing that more often. We'll have to invite your friends and your side of the family next time."

Yun's smile faded, then she gave a little smile and said, "Next time."

Soo Jin's door opened a crack. She ventured out, walking slowly, like an invalid.

Yun said, "Are you all right?"

Shin stared with interest from his perch on the couch.

Soo Jin said in a small voice, "I don't feel well."

Then she lurched toward the bathroom. In seconds we heard the sounds of puke splashing into the toilet, and a low groan from Soo Jin.

Yun looked at me, eyes flashing. "So you didn't fuck her?"

* * *

Yun walked around in a fury, looking for her car keys, muttering about morning sickness.

I sat on the sofa, wondering what the odds were. I fucked Soo Jin once—it had been a halfhearted fuck at that. I loved Soo Jin, but not the way a man loves a woman. Soo Jin didn't seem to occupy the same plain as so-called normal human beings. The truth was, I loved Soo Jin the way you love a dog. And now there might be a chance I was fathering a child with her.

Yun was back in fifteen minutes from Rite Aid with a home pregnancy kit. She disappeared into the bathroom with Soo Jin.

Shin was looking at me like he'd brought a checker set to a chess game. I could imagine him thinking the kidnapping was outrageous, the karaoke party unexpected, and Soo Jin's possible pregnancy too much to consider.

"Who are you?" asked Shin.

"What do you mean, 'Who am I'?"

"This blood feud has flowed like a river for many years," said Shin. "A white ghost like you marries Soo Jin, and the problems grow and grow. Where did you come from? Who sent you?"

"No one sent me. I'm not on a mission. I just want to work at my own business."

"Someone sent you," said Shin, not convinced. "Maybe there are more Nang than we realize."

I looked at the kids' toys scattered around the living room and imagined a third kid playing with them. A baby I'd had a hand in making. "For all I know there could be a million more

Nang. I never even heard the name until the night you blew that poor guy's head off in the Saja Room."

Shin said, "I don't believe you." Then he turned his face away, ending the conversation.

Yun came out of the bathroom trailing Soo Jin.

In Soo Jin's hand was a plastic stick—it looked like a toothbrush without bristles.

Yun pointed at the stick in Soo Jin's hands. "Your wife has something to tell you, Mr. Norgaard."

"C'mon, Yun," I complained. "Don't be like this."

"Two blue lines," said Yun.

"Does it mean what I think it means?" I asked.

Soo Jin said, "I'm pregnant."

A heavy feeling washed over me. If it was Yun's baby, maybe I'd feel different. If Soo Jin gave birth to a girl, the child would be safe from the blood feud—but only until it reached marrying age; then any serious suitor would be murdered by the Dokos. If Soo Jin gave birth to a boy, the target would be on the kid's back as soon as it was born, since it was the male children who carried on the family name.

I came out of my heavy thoughts to see Shin staring at me.

"You've made things worse," said Shin. "You've given birth to death."

I returned my version of his heavy stare and said, "Get over yourself, you pretentious fuck."

* * *

I poured a cup of coffee and went out back, dragging a lawn chair to a corner of the yard where no one could see me. I heard Yun's car reversing out of the drive as she headed off to work her shift. I needed some time to myself, to mull over this latest complication. I couldn't help feeling sorry for Soo Jin. In a perfect world, we'd be driving out to Babies "R" Us to look at cribs and rattles. Instead, Soo Jin had a husband who wasn't really a husband and a kid set to inherit a whole set of problems as soon as it was born.

My mind went back to what Ms. Tam had told me—that professionals were probably entering the picture. If I played this like a kidnapper in a movie, I was going to lose. I couldn't afford to fall into a predictable role. I couldn't be too easy to second-guess. If I was going to survive I was going to have to keep the Dokos off balance.

I went back into the house and into the kitchen where Shin was handcuffed to the pipe under the sink. That was the status quo—if he was out of my sight he had to be handcuffed. Otherwise I let him sit in the living room and think dark thoughts or watch TV, whatever he preferred.

His glare had softened into something less dark than hate, but still filled with loathing.

I got my phone out of my pocket and said to Shin, "I need a number."

* * *

Shin's brother, Sang-Yong, was crisp and controlled once he realized who was on the line. I explained to him that it was not my intention to hurt his brother, the honored patriarch of the Doko family. I didn't want a ransom. All I wanted was a signed declaration that would announce to the Korean community that the blood feud between the Doko and the Nang families had been settled to the satisfaction of all parties. I'd pay to post the declaration in the *Korea Times*. There would be an addendum to the declaration: that anyone not honoring the cessation of hostilities would bring great dishonor to their family.

I was laying it on a little thick, but I figured a three-hundred-year-old blood feud deserved the inflated language of a peace treaty.

Sang-Yong had listened carefully and then made a polite request that I remain on the line. I had no idea who he was talking to, but when he came back he said, "We will give you our answer tomorrow. Call us at the end of the day. Five."

Would it work? I had no idea. But it was better than hunkering down, waiting for the next shoe to drop. I had a feeling they knew exactly where I was. They'd seen me picking up Yun's kids. For all I know, some nosy Korean saw me and Yun dancing at Warsaw Wash, or eating oysters at the farmers' market. Once they set to connecting the dots with a vengeance, it was going to be easy for them to figure where I went to ground. The Dokos knew I witnessed firsthand how ruthless they could be. Maybe the only thing holding them back was the fear that if they backed me into a corner I'd do something final to the grand old man of the Doko clan.

Like blow his head off with a shotgun.

FORTY

When Yun returned home that evening she wouldn't look me in the eye. Instead she began preparing dinner, calling out to Soo Jin to help her. Soo Jin emerged from her room and drifted into the kitchen.

Yun handed her a mandoline and a couple of onions and said, "Slice these."

Watching from the kitchen doorway, I asked, "Do you need any help?"

Yun didn't answer right away. Eventually she said, "You can set the table."

I caught Shin watching me from his chair in the living room. I thought I could see a slight smile on his face, as though he was enjoying my discomfort.

As I set the table, I listened to Yun giving Soo Jin some advice on how to deal with her pregnancy.

"First of all, you're not going to be puking forever," said Yun. "That's going to go away. Keep a couple of saltines by the bed at all times. You eat those first thing—before you even get up. You're going to be hungry all the time, but don't eat like a pig. Lots of women use this as an excuse to eat chocolate, ice cream, doughnuts—all that crap. I have a juicer. You're going to drink fresh beet juice until your pee turns purple. It's good for your blood. Remember, what's good for you is good for the baby. I made an appointment with a doctor, first thing in the morning, tomorrow. We've got to make sure you're in good shape. Do you take any pills?"

"No," answered Soo Jin.

"I've never seen you smoke or drink."

"I never smoke," said Soo Jin.

"Well, don't drink, either," said Yun. "Not while you're pregnant."

"What about Frappuccinos?"

"A fetus doesn't need a caffeine buzz," answered Yun. "Think about it. That little baby is depending on you."

Soo Jin blinked as she sliced the onions.

Yun surprised me by giving Soo Jin a kiss on the cheek and saying, "You're gonna do fine."

* * *

That night, lying in bed with Yun, I made an attempt to explain.

"I should have told you the truth," I said, my head on the pillow, looking straight up at the ceiling. "But it was only one time with Soo Jin, and it was before you and I got together. I guess I was feeling like a married man. We were drinking champagne. With you, sex is wild. With Soo Jin—I don't know—it was more like mailing a letter."

"You should have told me," said Yun. "It made me feel stupid, finding out like that."

"You're right. I guess I thought I could ignore it, since it was never going to happen again."

"That's what you say now," countered Yun. "Wait until she has your baby."

"Soo Jin is like a baby herself. I'm going to need your help."

"I don't want to be your helper."

I tried wrapping my head around that statement and drew a blank.

I asked, "You don't want to help me?"

"Not that, you idiot," laughed Yun. "I don't want to be your helper. I want to be your wife."

"You are my wife," I said. "My real wife. We don't need a piece of paper. You're the one I love."

"You love me?" asked Yun.

"What'd I just say?"

"Say it again."

"Yeah, I guess I do." I felt light as a feather, and shining. I'd never said that to anybody. "I do love you. I just never said it out loud."

"I love you, too," said Yun.

The lightness in my heart kept expanding. I realized that was the first time anyone had ever told me they loved me.

* * *

The next morning, with Yun and Soo Jin at the doctor, I sat at the dining room table and checked my banking online. Warsaw Wash was doing fine. More money was coming in than going out.

Shin sat in the living room, watching cartoons with Mi-Cha and Tae-Yong. No matter how angry Shin might be, he was still programmed to be a grandfather. I saw him reach out with his left hand and steady Tae-Yong when it looked as though he would take a tumble.

I powered off my iPad. I was hoping that Yun wouldn't be too long—today was my day to go to the clinic, to have blood withdrawn. I was curious what Royal would have to say. I'd been checking through the newspapers, and there was nothing about Shin Doko being kidnapped. I wondered how Shin's disappearance was handled at the clinic, whether they suspected foul play or if they thought Shin had bailed midway through his visit.

It was close to eleven when Yun and Soo Jin returned.

Yun gave me a kiss and said softly, "Come with me. We have to talk."

I followed her into the bedroom.

Yun said, "The reason we were so long is because we did a blood test. It's not a hundred percent, but it's close."

"A test for what?"

"They have a new blood test called Pink or Blue," answered Yun. "Instead of having to wait until an ultrasound, they can tell really early on whether it's going to be a boy or girl."

"Tell me it's going to be a girl."

Yun shook her head. "She's gonna have a boy."

I let out a sigh.

I grabbed my forehead and began pacing, saying over and over, "Oh, man."

"You can't unring a bell," said Yun. "And you rang her bell real good. You made a boy."

"The Doko are going to kill me," I said. "And then they'll come for my son. This is all too sick."

For a moment I had a fantasy of executing Shin and then going after the other Dokos, one by one—until there was none left. Now it was my family they were fucking with, my own flesh and blood.

"You're supposed to call them today, right?" asked Yun.

"Yeah," I said. "They're going to tell me if they're willing to cease and desist."

Yun laid a hand on my shoulder. "Maybe a few hours from now this whole thing will be over."

"I can hope," I said.

* * *

I sat in the examination room, waiting on Royal. When he came through the door, instead of the frown I was expecting, he had a huge smile on his face.

"Wow," I said. "You look happy."

Royal extended his left hand with his fingers pointing down and said, "What do you think?"

There was a wedding band on his ring finger.

"You got married?"

"It was a long and miserable relationship but a whirlwind courtship," said Royal. "Walter came back. He heard around town that I was back in action—thanks to you—and he had a change of heart. He decided he couldn't live without me."

"Congratulations," I said. "That's great news."

"Yes," said Royal. "I went back to Rage the next night, and I was making quite the impression. All of a sudden I felt a hand on my shoulder, and I looked around and there was Walter, looking like one of those big-eyed children in the paintings. He said, 'We have to talk.' That's all it took. We were always meant for each other—it just took him time to realize it."

"You got married quick."

"When you're as old as I am there's not a minute to waste."

"Let me ask you a question," I said. "Is two guys getting married the same as a man and woman? I mean, the same forms and stuff?"

"Exactly the same, which makes it so beautiful. I would have loved to have had my family there for the ceremony, but they're still trying to get used to the fact that I'm gay. In their eyes I'm a sinner, so it would be too much for them to accept that I'm now a married man. I hope they eventually come around, but if they don't—too bad. I have a right to be happy."

"Well, if I make it through the next couple of days, I'm inviting you over for dinner. I'd like to meet Walter."

"Tell me what happened," whispered Royal. "Without actually telling me, if you know what I mean."

"Everything is in negotiation."

Royal picked up the needle to withdraw blood and said, "That's a good thing, right?"

FORTY-ONE

Yun had taken the rest of the day off. She and Soo Jin we're in the kitchen preparing an early dinner, a traditional Korean dish called bibimbap, kind of a sunny-side-up egg concoction where the yolks were broken and then mixed up with beef, chili paste, and all kinds of vegetables. Shin was sitting at the dining room table ramrod-straight in anticipation of a good meal.

I asked him, "You want a beer?"

He gave a curt nod, and I poured us both a glass of Hite. I sat down at the table with him. In twenty minutes I was to call Shin's brother to hear whether they accepted my terms for a truce.

Shin jerked his chin in the direction of Yun and said, "She's the one. She's your woman. Not the other."

"I guess you could say that," I said. "You've seen Yun in action. She's quite a woman."

"I know her family," said Shin.

"I haven't met them yet. You could say we've both been preoccupied."

"You could walk away from Soo Jin," said Shin. "She's not your woman."

"That's not going to happen."

"I could get you money. No one would have to die."

"It's too late," I said. "We're a strange family. But we're a family. We can't go throwing people overboard chasing a payday."

Shin asked, "What was your family like?"

"We weren't like you Koreans," I said. "We may have started off as immigrants, but we had no sense of tradition. We were

Norwegian but you'd never know it. I've never been to Norway, but from what I hear, Norwegians keep to themselves. My family took it a step further—my mom and dad didn't even socialize with their kids. So this blood feud business you're embroiled in is like something from another world."

"We need maps in life," said Shin. "They tell us where to go, but more importantly, they tell us where we've been."

"The thing about a map," I said. "It shows a lot of possible twists and turns going forward. You Dokos are acting like the trail in front of you is the same as the one behind you—set in stone."

"For us it is," said Shin.

"It's not set in stone for me," I said. "It's not something I set out to prove, but I'm proving it every day."

Shin took a sip of beer. Gave me a measured look. "You've made one misstep after another."

"There's an old saying," I said. "'You go your way, I'll go mine.' I think that's how it's going to have to be."

"Your way may not lead very far into the future," said Shin.

"Let's see what your brother says."

I got up and walked into the kitchen. Yun was stir-frying some vegetables. I gave her a kiss on the back of the neck that gave her chills.

I said, "It's time I made that call."

* * *

I sat outside at the patio table, my cell in front of me. Jamjari was laid out prone at my feet. He was a good dog. He was beginning to depend on me for his water and food; this made me pack leader in his eyes. When my cell showed exactly five o'clock I picked it up and called Shin's brother, Sang-Yong.

He picked up with a simple, "Yes?"

"This is Wes Norgaard," I said. "During our last call I gave you terms on how we could end this."

"Yes, you did."

"What have you decided?"

Sang-Yong said, "This is our answer..."

In the same fraction of time I heard the crack of the rifle and felt the pain of the bullet. I sprawled across the flagstones of the patio, scrambling toward the sliding glass door. Jamjari was on his feet, letting out a deep grunting bark.

Two more shots were fired. These missed, but one bullet shattered a flagstone, sending a shard of slate into my eye. I scurried into the house like a crab with a hot poker up its ass. Jamjari was behind me—if I was any slower he'd knock me down.

Yun was right there. She pulled me inside as a fourth shot shattered the glass of the patio door. I flung the curtains shut and yelled, "Get the kids in the bathroom. Make them lie down in the tub." Yun hurried the kids off to what I hoped was safety.

"Soo Jin," I yelled. "Close all the curtains and shades."

Shin sat like a statue. The best I can say for him is he didn't seem to enjoy seeing my family terrified.

I pointed at Shin and commanded Jamjari, "Watch that motherfucker."

Jamjari seemed to understand, since he sat on his haunches and stared at Shin.

With the windows covered I hurried into the bedroom and got my sawed-off. I loaded it and put a box of shells in my pocket. There was blood in the corner of my eye, but I could still see. The first shot had creased my side and my arm where it was pressed against my body. I lifted up my shirt—I was bleeding but it wasn't serious.

My knees started shaking in a delayed reaction. I waited for another shot but none came. I heard my phone ringing outside on the patio table.

Let it ring.

* * *

I sat on the edge of the tub with my shirt off as Yun cleaned my wounds with peroxide. There was a look of anguish on her face that was out of proportion to the severity of my injuries. I wanted to tell her everything would be all right. But we both knew that would be a lie. I remembered what Ms. Tam said about the Dokos sending professionals to kill me. That's what this ambush felt like. It was more than a bunch of clueless Koreans in an orange Rubicon.

I had one ear cocked for the police, but they never came. We were only a couple of blocks from Pico Boulevard, where Mexican gangs supplied frequent bursts of gunfire. You got used to it—in the morning you checked your car for bullet holes and went about your business.

I'd swallowed three extra-strength Excedrin, and the pain was minimal.

"It's not that bad," I said. "I got hurt worse falling off my bike when I was a kid."

"Stop it," Yun said. "Don't be an asshole."

Yun taped some gauze bandages in place and then peered into my eye.

"How's it look?" I asked.

"I'm pissed," she said. "They could have killed you."

"That was the general idea," I said.

"You love me?" asked Yun.

"Yeah, I do. A lot."

I touched the Band-Aid over my eye. "How's the eye?"

Yun touched the side of my head. "Just a scratch under your eyebrow."

"I feel like I'm using up my share of luck."

Yun capped the peroxide. "This has gone far enough."

"You've got a plan?"

"No. I've got something to say. Come with me."

I put my shirt back on and followed Yun. She picked up the handcuff key from a peg on the wall and freed Shin. He stood up—you could almost hear his bones creak. He wouldn't look me in the eye. If I didn't know him better I'd think he was ashamed of having our house shot up. Any one of those bullets could have slammed into Mi-Cha or Tae-Yong.

Yun called out, "Soo Jin…"

Soo Jin came out of the spare bedroom.

Yun went into the living room, where the kids were sitting on the rug watching TV. She picked up the remote and thumbed it off.

"All of you, sit down," said Yun.

I sat down on the sofa. Soo Jin sat next to me, and Shin took his customary seat in the easy chair.

I said to Yun, "What's going on?"

Yun cocked a finger like it was a gun and pointed it at Shin. "This has gone on long enough."

Shin stuck out his chin. "Do not talk to me that way."

"Wes," said Yun. "Do you really think you can hide in Koreatown with no one knowing?"

"I don't know," I said. "You tell me."

"Maybe it could be done," said Yun. "If you didn't sing karaoke in the Saja Room every night, if you didn't wash cars in a K-Town car wash, if you didn't drive around with me."

I didn't like the sound of this. "What are you getting at?"

"The day you kidnapped Shin, the Doko family knew exactly where he was taken. They knew he would be safe. The day you moved in with me, they knew."

Soo Jin was looking frightened.

I placed my hand on Soo Jin's hand and asked, "Are you OK?"

"I had a feeling," said Soo Jin. "But I wasn't sure."

"Wes, I told you I love you," said Yun. "I'm not afraid to say it in front of anyone. I love you."

I glanced at Shin and then back at Yun. "I love you, too."

Shin spat out a bunch of Korean words at Yun.

Yun bristled, and I asked her, "What did Shin say?"

"He warned me not to bring dishonor to my family."

"Who the fuck cares what he thinks?"

"I do," said Yun. "I'm his granddaughter. I'm a Doko."

FORTY-TWO

Hearing this bombshell, I got off the couch and said to Shin, "Get your ass in the kitchen."

I handcuffed him to the pipe under the sink.

The house seemed small. Probably because I didn't dare leave.

I looked at Yun, where she stood in the living room. My heart was heavy. I didn't know what to think. Finally I said, "I've got a kid coming. I need to know what the fuck is going on."

"I wanted to help."

"Who? Me?"

"Yeah, you," said Yun. "When you married Soo Jin, I got scared for you," said Yun. "I thought if I kept you close I could keep them from hurting either one of you."

"Was that bullet meant to kill me?"

"Of course they were trying to kill you," said Yun. "But they didn't tell me what they were going to try and do. I didn't know anything about it. I kept telling my family, 'Wait, wait—I know he's going to leave Soo Jin.' But they must have found out about Soo Jin being pregnant. I don't know how—maybe the doctor told them. Once my family heard she was going to have a boy, I guess they decided they couldn't wait any longer."

It was making me crazy hearing Yun refer to the Dokos as her family.

My mind was filled with the kinds of thoughts a fourteen-year-old girl writes in her diary. Does she love me? Was it all a lie? One minute I'm running around with a sawed-off shotgun; the next I'm pondering the vagaries of true love.

"Soo Jin," I said. "Please take care of the kids." I pointed at Yun. "You. In the bedroom."

I walked into the bedroom and threw the covers back on the bed and started unbuttoning my shirt. Yun saw what I was up to and closed the door behind her.

"I don't know what to think," I said. "So, for a half hour or so, I'm not going to."

Yun toed off her shoes and then pulled her T-shirt over her head. Her bra straps cut into the soft flesh of her shoulders. Her belly was a sexy curve all its own.

She watched me pull off my jeans and pull down my underwear. Her watching me—looking at my cock—was always a turn-on, and I was already hard. She came over to me and laid her head on my shoulder. I wrapped my arms around her. Her skin was a lovely butterscotch color, smooth to the touch.

I kissed her neck, and she pulled me down onto the bed.

* * *

Fucking Yun wasn't a magic carpet ride to the truth, but it cleared out some of the jimjams.

Lying back on the pillow next to her, I said, "Simple question. Are you with me, or the Dokos?"

"What do you think?"

"I think you're with me. The problem is I don't know what to do. If I go about my business, I'm a dead man. I could hide, but you've told me this whole hiding thing was bullshit—they always knew where to find me."

"They won't kill me," said Yun. "They won't kill you if you get a divorce. They won't kill Soo Jin—she's a woman. But they'll kill her boy."

I rubbed my temples with both hands, trying to ward off a headache. "My boy."

Yun placed her hand on my arm. "I'll help you fight."

"Do you think they still have a shooter out there?"

"Probably not," said Yun. "After those shots they'd be afraid the police would come. But I'm sure they're watching the house."

"Aren't they afraid I'll hurt Shin?"

"They're praying you won't hurt him."

Yun reached for her jeans where they were draped on a chair by the side of the bed. She dug out her cell phone.

She held up a finger to keep me quiet as she got Sang-Yong on the phone. "He's alive...The white ghost. Shin is unharmed. I'll make sure Shin is OK. But you have to give me a night to calm things down...Everything is crazy here right now. If you come back tonight, I can't promise I can protect Shin. I'll call you tomorrow."

Yun placed the phone on the chair and leaned back on the pillow. I had a feeling I'd never get tired of looking at her face.

"So what are we going to do?" asked Yun.

"This stupid blood feud has rules," I said. "These frozen fucks like to follow the rules. The rules are the rules are the rules. That's the kind of stubborn attitude that had the Dokos honor-bound to settle the score, even if it took three hundred years."

"That's how we are," said Yun.

"They kill as many guys as they can, but they don't ever kill women, right?"

"Right."

"And when a woman marries, she gives up her family name and takes her husband's name."

"Even more than that," said Yun. "The wife loses all the family heritage she was born with. If I was to marry you, I wouldn't be a Doko anymore."

"Get dressed," I said. "I'm letting Shin go."

"But why?"

"I don't need him anymore."

FORTY-THREE

I handed Shin a bottle of rubbing alcohol and a paper towel. "This should take the tape residue off your hands."

Shin looked at me with suspicion.

Soo Jin came into the kitchen and said, "You're letting him go?"

"Yeah," I said. "There's no sense in keeping him. Not anymore."

"What about Yun? She's a Doko."

"Everything is in a state of flux," I said. "I'll fill you in later."

Soo Jin walked over to the kitchen counter, to a wooden block with four knives sticking out of slots. She withdrew the largest knife and pointed it at Shin.

"I ought to stab you in the heart," said Soo Jin. "That way you can't see us suffer. You'll never know what happened to my baby."

I didn't know Soo Jin all that well, but I knew she didn't have the heart to hurt a soul, let alone Shin.

"I wish this was over," said Shin. "But it can't be stopped. It has to be settled."

I took the knife away from Soo Jin and put it back into the block. "I agree. We're going to honor our ancestors. My ancestors were Vikings. We're going to chew it up and spit it out, just like Sinatra."

I took my phone out of my pocket and punched in a number. "LA City Cab? I need you to send a car over to pick up a friend of mine. No, I don't know where he's going. He'll tell you. You need an address? Let's just say he's going to Koreatown."

* * *

We took my Jeep Cherokee, but Yun drove; after all, she was the pro. The desert highway at night was a joy after the events of the day. Empty. No billboards. No lights. Just stars in the sky and a blurred-out landscape.

Soo Jin sat in the back with the kids. Jamjari lay down in the back compartment. Every once in a while he'd lift his head and then go back to sleep.

I fiddled with the radio dial and found a Mexican station. I was sick of Korea and sick of myself. Mexican music suited me just fine.

Soo Jin spoke up from the back seat. "Where are we going?"

I said, "You ever hear of Reno?"

"No," answered Soo Jin. "Why are we going there?"

"Simple," I said. "You and me are getting a divorce."

* * *

It was almost dawn when we checked in to the Old 40 West Motel. I didn't think the Dokos would find us here—at least not in the two or three days we'd need to seal the deal. We got a pet-friendly room with two queen-size beds. The kids slept with Soo Jin, and I curled up next to Yun. I'd set my phone to wake me up in two hours, and I think the short leash gave me weird dreams. Drowning dreams, with my foot jammed between sea rocks and the tide slowly rising. Ugly dreams.

When I got up I stumbled into the bathroom and unpeeled the paper from the tiny bar of soap, and washed my face in a sink that was a hair away from falling off the wall. Yun came in and said, "I'm going with you."

We drove down Lincoln Highway. Reno was an abomination; but I never liked casino towns. One short visit to Las Vegas three years ago had cured me of any fascination I might have for the gambling life. When you started counting up the sour faces on busted gamblers trudging through the casinos, the ratio of losers to winners was a hundred to one. Odds like those were a loser's game.

The visit at Wilson Attys. was quick. Discretion and cash were a great combination. I now had an imaginary six-week residency in Reno, enough to push through a divorce in the next twenty-four hours.

* * *

Mi-Cha pushed the chicken croquette around her plate. I think she was more accustomed to Chicken McNuggets.

I said, "Try a little ketchup."

"I taste pepper," said Mi-Cha.

"Don't be so fussy," said Yun. "It's food."

Mi-Cha took a second bite and decided she liked it.

The Reno diner wasn't fancy, but it would serve its purpose—getting us filled with cheap food before the six-hour drive back to LA.

The quickie divorce had gone through like grease through a goose. Maybe because of this, I noticed Soo Jin looking glum, ignoring her bacon cheeseburger.

"Are you all right?" I asked.

"I don't know," answered Soo Jin.

"We're still a family," I said.

"But I'm pregnant," said Soo Jin. "You're not my husband anymore."

"We're going to fix that, don't worry," I said.

Yun reached out and laid a hand on Soo Jin's forearm. "It's going to be all right, really."

Soo Jin didn't seem convinced.

"I love our son already," I said. "No one's going to mess with him, and no one's going to mess with you, or Yun." I pointed at Mi-Cha and Tae-Yong. "Or those kids."

Mi-Cha said, "What about Jamjari?"

I looked out of the window, at Jamjari sitting in the front seat of my Jeep Cherokee.

"Jamjari, too," I said. "We're a family. We're going to stick together."

FORTY-FOUR

It was three in the morning when we got back to LA. We didn't dare go to Yun's house. I took a flier and called Jules.

He answered on the fifth ring. "Who is this? Do you know what time it is?"

"Jules, it's me—Wes."

His voice softened. "You all right?"

"Mostly very good. I think I have the Koreans by the balls. But they don't know that and they're gunning for me."

"You in trouble right now?"

"No, we're OK."

"What's the 'we' stuff?"

"I got a question for you. Are you or your wife allergic to dogs?"

* * *

A half hour later we were pulling up to Jules's house in Redondo Beach. Jules opened the door, dressed in a burgundy velour bathrobe, looking like a gangster in a Mafia movie.

I'd told Jules how many of us there were, but seeing us troop from the car up the steps made his jaw drop. Jamjari brought up the rear.

Jules asked, "Is that dog house trained?"

I said, "Yeah, he's good that way."

Once we were inside and the door was closed, I was face-to-face with Jules's wife for the first time.

"This is Mary," said Jules. "The rest of you, give her your name on your own time. Introductions are too much for me to deal with this time of night."

Mary was frail—she couldn't have been more than ninety pounds. Her gray hair was wispy, and she was dressed in a robe that matched the one Jules was wearing.

"Hi, Mary," I said. "It's good to finally meet you. Thanks for opening up your home on such short notice."

"Jules has told me about you—some of the awful things you're dealing with." Mary took my arm. "Come on into the living room."

Soo Jin and Yun sat on either side of me. The kids immediately sacked out on the carpet, using Jamjari as a pillow.

Jules said, "So, which one of you is the wife?"

I jumped in. "That's a good question. You see, we just got back from Reno." I pointed at Soo Jin. "We just got a quickie divorce."

"Excellent," said Jules. "You should have done that a long time ago. Now you can shake hands and go your separate ways. Problem solved."

"It's not that simple," I said. "You see, Soo Jin is pregnant."

Mary grimaced, as though she was having second thoughts about letting me in the door.

"You're confusing me," said Jules.

"I admit, it's confusing," I said. "But it'll all make sense pretty soon. Especially after tomorrow's wedding."

Yun pointed at her chest. "You're gonna marry me?"

"Let me explain," I said.

* * *

Around five, Yun, Soo Jin, and the kids moved into the spare bedroom to catch a few hours of sleep. Jules—dressed now—said, "C'mon. It's been years since I saw the sun come up on the beach."

On the drive over we grabbed coffee from a Dunkin' Donuts. The sky was starting to lighten at the edges when we made it to the sand. The tide was low, and gentle breakers were foaming white fifty feet from shore.

"I used to come out here a couple times a week to catch the sunrise," said Jules. "It always set me up real good for a day's work."

"I can feel it," I said.

"So I get the Soo Jin connection," said Jules. "But what's with the other one, Yun?"

"She's my girlfriend."

"And Soo Jin is good with that?"

"Soo Jin was never my wife wife, if you know what I mean."

"Right," said Jules. "You married her and knocked her up, but why call her a wife?"

"We had sex once, that's all," I said. "I wasn't looking to be a father, but now that I have a son on the way, I kind of like the idea."

"You're lucky you made the deal for Warsaw Wash before all this rigmarole," said Jules. "If I knew you were this convoluted with broads, I probably wouldn't have gone through with it."

The sand was going from dark-gray to brown as the horizon took on a glow.

"How's Mary feeling?" I said. "I didn't expect to meet her."

"She has her good days and bad days. Your group bursting in livened the place up. She's going to talk my ear off after you're gone. Especially about this gambit you have planned."

"Think it'll work?"

"I tried to poke holes in it and it held up," said Jules, as he stepped away from a breaking wave. "You really think you can put it together so fast?"

"Cash worked magic in Reno, pushing through a divorce," I said. "I figure it can work the same kind of magic arranging a quick wedding."

A curve of bright sun showed on the horizon. Jules stopped and stared.

"Hallelujah," said Jules. "Here comes another day."

FORTY-FIVE

The first call I made was to the Wilshire Christian Church. Yun had told me that most of the Dokos were Christian, and that was their preferred place of worship. I'd been by the building a hundred times. While I wasn't a churchgoer, it was an impressive piece of architecture: a mash-up between Mexican and medieval.

It took three phone calls until I connected with the congregation president. I got his attention when I told him I wanted to book a wedding in one of their chapels. His ears really pricked up when I told him I also wanted to make a generous cash donation to the church, no strings attached. He hemmed and hawed about propriety and protocol, but we both knew the deal was good as done. When I told him exactly what I wanted there was a pause on the line, and then a quick, "That won't be a problem."

We settled on a time. Five o'clock this evening.

I was going to have to move fast.

* * *

I told Yun and Soo Jin, "We're going to have to go shopping for a wedding dress."

* * *

Jules's backyard was being warmed by the sun as the kids played fetch with Jamjari. The rest of us were sitting around a glass patio table. All except Mary—she was back in bed, probably wondering when this wave of invaders would recede.

I'd been on the phone all morning spreading the word about today's wedding and handing out invites: Manuel and the guys at the car wash, Royal, Kwan, Min Jee, and Ms. Tam. I told Ms. Tam to spread the word with the regulars at the Saja Room and let them know they were all invited. Soo Jin called her friends at the dumpling shop and the few remaining members of the Nang family.

Yun's calls were going to be the hardest—inviting the Doko clan. Before she got started I asked her if she'd mind if I called Shin myself.

"Only if you put it on speaker," she said.

"Good idea," said Jules. "I want to hear that motherfucker squirm."

I put the phone in the middle of the table. Shin's voice sounded harsh when he picked up and answered in Korean, "*Yoboseyo.*"

"Shin. It's me, Wes."

There was a pause, then: "What is it you want?"

"I'm driving a nail through this blood feud," I said. "I asked you to end this of your own free will. You wouldn't or you couldn't."

"I have nothing to say to a dead man."

"You've terrorized my family long enough. Dude, I'm going to put your head in the Mixmaster."

"Look at your hands," said Shin.

I looked at my hands; they were clean enough.

"You have the hands of a peasant," said Shin. "You wash cars. You're a nobody—*mee-cheen-nom.*"

Jules leaned toward the phone. "Hey, fuck you, Shin."

I waved Jules to quiet down.

"Who was that?" asked Shin.

"It was nothing," I said. "As far as me being a *mee-cheen-nom,* whatever that is, so be it. I barely made it through high school.

I'm not much smarter than the next guy, which is fine with me. But I pay my own way, and I don't fuck people over."

Jules gave me a look and whispered, "That's the best you can do for a comeback? Let me talk to the fucking snake."

I put up a hand to silence Jules and said into the phone, "I have a reason for this call. I have a function I'd like you to attend at the Wilshire Christian Church. I chose the Wilshire because I know you go there every Sunday. I'm inviting you to a wedding. Five o'clock. Don't bother with a present."

Jules leaned close and said with a smile, "Your presence is your present, motherfucker."

The line went dead.

I looked at Yun. "Do you think he'll come?"

"He'll be there," said Yun. "With five bodyguards."

I put my phone in my pocket. "Shin wouldn't shoot up a church, would he?"

"Up until 'I do' anything could happen," said Yun.

* * *

We said our good-byes to Jules and Mary and told them we'd see them at the ceremony. I was still afraid of heading back to Yun's so we booked a room for one night at the Ramada Wilshire, a short distance from the church. We were going to need a base for all the primping and prodding that would be going on.

By two o'clock, through a combination of luck and under-the-table cash payments, we had all the documents we needed. I peeled off in one direction and the women in another. At first I thought of renting a tuxedo but decided it would be a waste of money. It would be smarter buying a new suit. I picked one off the rack at the Target in West Hollywood and was in and out of the door in twenty minutes, loaded down with new shoes, socks, a dress shirt, tie, and belt. When I got back to the hotel room Yun and Soo Jin and the kids were still out.

I sacked out on the hotel bed, exhausted. It had been a long time since I pulled an all-nighter. I would have drifted off to sleep if my phone hadn't buzzed. I picked it up and heard Royal's voice.

"Wes," he said. "I got your message. You sounded so excited."

"Listen, I know this is short notice," I said. "But I have a feeling you have a healthy respect for the dramatic."

"Yes, I do."

"Are you free this evening, say five o'clock?"

"I'm free."

"Do you have a clean suit?"

"Of course I have a clean suit."

"How would you like to be best man at a wedding?"

"Oh, dear," said Royal. "Tell me more."

* * *

I sat across from Soo Jin in a small antechamber outside the entrance to the wedding chapel. I wasn't one for churches. As soon as I was old enough to assert my own power—eight years old—I stopped going. Even so, it was a pleasant room to hide away in. The walls of the antechamber were high-grade stucco, with dark-mahogany baseboards and crown molding. The benches we sat on were made of the same polished wood. On the wall was a crudely carved and painted Jesus on the cross; it looked like something found in a barn in Mexico. Even though I wasn't religious, I would have liked to have hung it in my own home—it was an honest piece of work.

Soo Jin looked beautiful in a white wedding dress a lot more fancy than the one she wore when she married me in Ms. Tam's apartment. It cost more than a thousand bucks, but it was worth it. My wallet had taken a real hit the last couple of days. If I succeeded every dime would be well spent. If I failed we wouldn't have much capital to keep the fight going.

I smiled at Soo Jin. "You make a beautiful bride."

"I don't want to be a bride anymore."

"Lots of twists and turns. Maybe too many."

"I was never divorced before," said Soo Jin.

I thought of her five husbands who had been murdered by the Dokos. I bet all five wish they'd had a chance to file.

I got up and opened the door a crack. There were still some stragglers filing in. I recognized Ramon from the car wash and a few regulars from the Saja Room.

I sat back down. Soo Jin's hands were smoothing the dress where it lay over her thighs, over and over again.

"Don't be nervous," I said.

"I can't help it."

"Your life is going to change in a good way," I said.

"I hope so."

I figured I should try to distract her. "What would you do if you could do anything?"

"I don't want much," said Soo Jin. "I liked making dumplings. Maybe I can get my job back after our baby is born."

It was strange, hearing the words *our baby*.

I said, "You've been good with Mi-Cha and Tae-Yong."

Soo Jin smiled but didn't say anything.

"I think they love you a lot," I said.

"That's good," said Soo Jin. "It will make everything easier."

There was a knock at the door.

I said, "Come in."

The door opened, and an usher from the church poked his head inside. Mi-Cha was beside him, dressed as a flower girl. "You can come out now," said the usher. "All the guests have been seated. When you hear the music cue—the wedding march—we'll open the door and you'll give Mi-Cha a minute, and then you'll follow down the aisle."

Soo Jin and I stood up. Soo Jin couldn't be any more nervous than me—I definitely had the butterflies. I had a lot of friends on the other side of the door, and a lot of enemies, too. I wondered if the wedding march would have the opposite effect than intended—instead of commencing a wedding it would be like ringing the bell at a prizefight. I had the .38 Special tucked in my belt, behind my back and under my jacket. Carrying a pistol under any circumstances felt strange—it felt doubly strange packing iron in a church. When Jules heard I was leaving my sawed-off behind, he asked if he could bring it along, just in case. I think he was playing out a fantasy in his mind, but I gave it to him anyway. He'd showed me a box that had held long-stemmed roses—the perfect size for carrying the shotgun. I agreed with him that it wouldn't raise any eyebrows while he was sitting in a pew at a wedding.

I looked over at Soo Jin. Maybe it was my imagination, but she looked more mature and womanly than when I'd first met her a few weeks ago. Part of me loved her a lot.

I took Soo Jin by the hand. "You ready for this?"

"I hope my family understands," said Soo Jin.

"If they don't, that's their problem."

Soo Jin smiled. The smile turned into a grimace of panic when we heard the opening bars of "Bridal Chorus."

I squeezed her hand. "You can do this."

The chapel door slowly swung open, and Mi-Cha began her measured walk down the aisle.

Soo Jin and I took a step closer and saw that the chapel was packed; at first it was a blur of people.

One person stood out.

At the end of the aisle, standing on the altar, was Yun, Soo Jin's bride. Thank God that California allowed gays to marry—even if they were heterosexual. Yun looked gorgeous in a scoop-necked wedding dress tricked out in lace and satin. Yun caught my eye and gave me a radiant smile. For a second I felt a pang and wished I was up there on the altar exchanging wedding vows with her, instead of Soo Jin.

Royal stood next to Yun as her best man. He was dressed in a green sharkskin suit and was beaming a smile at me. I'd have to thank him later. It was his impending gay marriage to Walter that had given me the idea that Soo Jin and Yun should get hitched. With them being married, the idiotic three-hundred-year-old blood feud would come to a screeching halt. If the Doko and Nang families kept it up they'd be killing themselves. It would be like punching yourself in the face.

I took Soo Jin by the arm and slowly walked down the aisle, glancing from side to side. Manuel, dressed in a sharp-looking suit, flashed me a gang sign. Jules gave me a nod and then pointed at the flower box next to him on the pew. I saw Ms. Tam and Kwan and lots of familiar faces and some I'd never seen. I figured the ones wearing heavy scowls were Doko family members, here as witnesses rather than celebrants.

Halfway down the aisle I saw Shin looking over his shoulder at me. The motherfucker was sitting in the front row, flanked by bodyguards. He looked like he wanted to rip me apart with his teeth. Up until the last moment, Shin must have thought I was the one who was going to marry Yun. Maybe he didn't like the thought, but my marrying Yun would signal I was ready to turn my back on Soo Jin and our son. But seeing Soo Jin in a wedding dress—walking toward the altar to exchange vows with Yun—was evidently blowing Shin's mind. I wasn't sure, but I thought I could see spittle at the corner of his mouth.

The priest standing next to Yun was Asian, probably Korean. He looked uncomfortable, like he wanted to be done and gone.

I stopped at the end of the aisle. Soo Jin squeezed my hand and whispered, "I'm frightened."

I gave her a kiss on the cheek. "You'll do fine. Don't worry."

The priest took a deep breath and said, "We are gathered together on this beautiful afternoon to share a deeply meaningful experience with Yun and Soo Jin as they exchange vows of their everlasting love."

A murmur went through the crowd.

The priest looked at me and said, "Who gives this woman to be married to this woman?"

"I do," I said.

Like a dad giving his daughter away, I placed Soo Jin's hand in Yun's. With my back to the people in the pews, I mouthed the words *I love you* to Yun. That got another smile out of her.

I took my place in the front row, on the other side of the aisle from Shin, next to Min Jee and the kids. I leaned over and said to Mi-Cha, "Your mommy is beautiful, isn't she."

"They're both beautiful," said Mi-Cha.

It was true. Yun was a force of nature, and Soo Jin looked like she had floated down from the spirit world.

The priest grimly plowed forward: "As Yun and Soo Jin take their vows today in holy matrimony, we are privileged to witness the joyous love of a new union uniting the Doko and Nang families."

I looked over at Shin when I heard this. He was looking straight ahead, his fists clenched on his knees. If Shin was a bottle rocket his fuse was lit and racing, throwing off sparks.

I saw the priest look down at Shin. It was clear the imminent explosion wasn't lost on him. "Much as the world looks forward to each new season of the year, Yun and Soo Jin look forward with joy to each season of their marriage," said the priest, looking nervous. "Yun and Soo Jin, by placing yourself in God's hands, your love for each other will grow deeper with every passing day. Even so, it's important to remember that to truly love and cherish another person you must be willing to embrace their strong points and their weak points, with equal measures of understanding and respect."

Shin jumped to his feet. The bodyguards stood up with Shin. I noticed the tall Korean looking back at me, still giving me the sneer.

My hand went under my coat, to the pistol in my belt, but I didn't draw.

Shin turned toward the people filling the pews and shouted, "The Doko family does not accept this union!"

Royal frowned and said to Shin, "Shame on you."

Lots of people were on their feet now; some looked ready to fight, others ready to flee.

Shin lurched toward Yun, reaching out to grab her hand. Yun took a step back, and Shin went flying into a pedestal topped with flowers, sending it crashing to the floor. Shin's bodyguards flowed onto the altar to retrieve their boss. The priest darted behind Soo Jin and Yun, looking like he wanted to be a million miles away.

I stood up and walked over to stand in front of Yun and Soo Jin. By that time, Shin was back on his feet. He looked a mess, with water from the vase dripping down his face.

I pointed a finger at him. "Get back in your seat. You don't decide what goes on here."

For a second it looked like I was going to be charged by Shin and his bodyguards. Royal came and stood by my side. I looked behind me and saw Yun take Soo Jin by the hand.

Shin noticed, and I could see the air deflate out of him. He wasn't stupid. He knew when he held a losing hand.

Shin turned and walked slowly down the aisle, followed by his bodyguards. Several others left with him, probably Dokos sympathetic to Shin's humiliation. The tall Korean put a comforting hand on Shin's shoulder, and the old man angrily shrugged it away.

The priest still hid behind Soo Jin and Yun.

I caught his eye and said, "You want to get this thing back on the rails?"

FORTY-SIX

The first couple of times Mi-Cha and I made pancakes, it had been a real mess. Water dripping down cabinets, pancake batter on our shoes, both of us gritty with flour. After a half dozen attempts we were getting the hang of it. We'd start the bacon sizzling and begin round after round of blueberry pancakes, heaping them on a platter in the oven to keep them warm, until we had enough to serve the whole family at once. Someone at school had told Mi-Cha about chocolate chip pancakes, but I was holding the line against that abomination.

I handed the ladle to Mi-Cha and said, "Your turn."

She concentrated hard as she held the ladle over the frying pan and poured four perfect pancakes.

"You are good," I said.

Yun came in from behind and gave me a hug. "When are you going to make them Korean style?"

"What would that be?"

"Mung bean flour with scallions and minced garlic."

"Breakfast?"

"I'll make them tonight," said Yun. "You'll love them."

It had been roughly twenty months since Yun and Soo Jin married. During that time I'd learned a lot about women. Half the battle was not trying to be right all the time. Instead I practiced the art of keeping my mouth shut and letting life flow over me, like I was an aerodynamic design undergoing testing. I'd only speak once I had a clear idea what it was I wanted to say. It was working for me.

After Shin had stomped out of the church we'd gotten on with the wedding. There had been some grumbling from the pews but no more outbursts. After a few more minutes of platitudes from the priest, Royal presented the gold wedding bands to Yun and Soo Jin, and they placed the bands on their ring fingers.

Life seemed to hang in the balance for a moment—then they shared a chaste kiss. Half the crowd cheered, and the other half sat on their hands.

After the ceremony Ms. Tam had invited all of us back to the Saja Room to celebrate the wedding. Maybe she was being bold and magnanimous; maybe she was trying to recoup lost business. Either way, the Hite and soju were flowing. We all sang, even Soo Jin. She surprised me with a tender rendition of "Be My Baby" delivered in either my direction or Yun's—it was hard to tell, since I had my arm around Yun's waist and her chin was on my shoulder.

On one of my trips back from the bathroom, Ms. Tam was waiting for me in the narrow corridor. She blocked my way and said, "I got a call from one of the Dokos. He told me Shin was done. The feud is over for good."

"Are you sure?"

"As sure as I can be, without hearing it from Shin himself."

"What if I don't want it to end?"

Ms. Tam looked at me like I was crazy.

"No, really," I said. "What if I want to use this marriage to dismantle the Dokos from the inside? I could do it. I got this far. They won't know who their allies are—it will be family member against family member. If I come out swinging the Dokos won't even be Korean when I'm done—they'll be Norwegian."

Ms. Tam took a step back. "You'd do that?"

"Yeah, I would," I said. "If Shin ever fucks with my family again, I'll make sure his last years on earth are a living hell. Dokos will be dropping like flies. You tell him that."

Ms. Tam frowned, creasing her makeup. "I'll make sure he knows."

I went to move around her, and she blocked my way. "Everybody's been asking me," she said.

"Asking you what?"

"Are Soo Jin and Yun in love with each other? Are they doing it?"

I put a hand on Ms. Tam's shoulder and gently pushed her aside. A few steps down the corridor she called out, "Well are they?"

Without stopping, I said over my shoulder, "Yun's with me."

* * *

I scraped up the last of the pancake batter and handed the ladle to Mi-Cha. With great concentration she made a trio of silver-dollar pancakes. The family was waiting around the breakfast table. I brought the platter of pancakes over and laid it down on a hot plate.

Soo Jin had our baby in her arms.

Yun patted the seat of my chair. I have to admit, when the baby was born, I was pleased to see little Magnus Norgaard Doko sporting a shiny pair of blue eyes.

I sat down and forked a couple of pancakes onto my plate and poured a generous helping of molasses over them.

Warsaw Wash was paying the bills. I had my regulars—one of them was Shin Doko. Every Thursday he showed up in his black Lincoln. Some people might think I'd resent having Shin roll in for a wash.

It didn't bother me.

I like my job.

- THE END -

ABOUT THE AUTHOR

 Mark Rogers's career as a travel journalist has brought him to fifty-six countries and counting. These trips have fed his imagination and at the same time provided authentic experiences and sensory detail that find their way into his novels and screenplays. Mark's won multiple awards for his travel writing, including an award for his Hurricane Ivan coverage in Jamaica. His work regularly appears in *USA Today* and other media outlets. Mark lives in Baja California, Mexico, with his Sinaloa-born wife, Sophy, where they recently built a rock house overlooking the sea.

47224030R00139

Made in the USA
San Bernardino, CA
25 March 2017